M.T. DOHANEY

D0859125

A MARRIAGE OF MASKS

RAGWEED
THE ISLAND PUBLISHER

Cover art: Susan Wood, *Dress #12*, 1990, mixed media/paper,
185x121 cm. Collection of the Nova Scotia Art Bank.

Printed and bound in Canada by: Les Editions Marquis Ltée.

Ragweed Press acknowledges the generous support
of the Canada Council.

Published by:
Ragweed Press
P.O. Box 2023
Charlottetown, P.E.I.
Canada, C1A 7N7

Acknowledgements
The author wishes to thank her family for their
understanding and patience in allowing the final touching up of
this book to absorb much of her time during their Christmas
vacation. She also wishes to thank The Writer's Breakfast Group
of Fredericton for their comments during the workshopping
of this novel. Finally, she wishes to thank her editor,
Lynn Henry, for her insights and astute editing.

Canadian Cataloguing in Publication Data
Dohaney, M.T., date
    A marriage of masks

    ISBN 0-921556-56-X

I. Title.

PS8557.0257M37 1995   C813'.54   C95-950024-3
PR9199.3.D64M37 1995

We dance around in a ring and suppose,
But the secret sits in the middle and knows.
— ROBERT FROST

Contents

O n e

It is the Tuesday following Thanksgiving — almost the halfway mark in October. The traffic in downtown Fredericton is so heavy that as Laura Stevenson darts her chestnut-coloured Toyota in and out amongst cars, trucks and bicycles and heads for the TransCanada highway, she feels like a salmon bashing its way upstream. She silently chastises herself for not leaving home either earlier or later and avoiding this crush.

The hills surrounding Fredericton are a blaze of colour — sugar maple red, waterbirch yellow, pin cherry orange. The air is crisp and clear, and the sun is so bright that the aging elm trees lining the sidewalks glisten as if their leaves have been waxed and polished.

Laura loves autumn — especially autumn in New Brunswick. She thinks it's the melancholy of it. Dying leaves, lonely moons and starless skies are definitely to her liking. And she also relishes thoughts of cold nights under heavy blankets. She used to think that if she ever fell in love again, it would be in October.

As she eases into the last exit lane and sees a stretch of clear driving ahead, she throws a quick, sideways glance at her daughter, Hannah, who is fused to the passenger door as if she wants to put as much distance as possible between her and her mother. Hannah sits at an angle and stares sulkily at the Saint John River. Her crimp-curled blond hair whips out through the open window and catches the sunlight, reminding Laura of Rumpelstiltskin's mound of golden flax.

Hannah had been home for the Thanksgiving weekend, and if she had been able to find any way of getting back to Laval University other than driving with her mother, she would have jumped at the offer.

Laura knows this, but understands. The weekend just past had not been one for strengthening familial bonds — particularly bonds between mother and daughter. Laura thinks, although perhaps a trifle unfairly, that this is mostly Kevin's fault. Kevin, husband of Laura and father of Hannah — and, for the past several years, Chairman of the Sociology Department at the same university where he was once a green graduate student — had decided that sooner was better than later to tell Hannah that her parents' marriage was about to capsize. Of course, the marriage had been foundering for at least two decades, but because Laura and Kevin believed the foundering had taken place unbeknownst to Hannah, they were certain the news would come as a terrible jolt to her.

Laura had wanted to hold off the telling. She had felt it would spoil Hannah's Thanksgiving. Kevin, however, had replied that this was just Laura's way of trying to avoid the unpleasant. He had used the words "evasive tactics," injuring her with social science jargon — a longtime habit of his that is probably not deliberate, but nevertheless very effective. He had pointed out that there would always be a holiday to spoil. If it wasn't Thanksgiving, it would be Christmas, or Easter or a birthday, or the Feast of St. Blaise or National Pickle Week. He had said that the quicker Hannah was told about how things really were, the better off she'd be. It would give her time to adjust to the news before the Christmas examinations came upon her. And, besides, he had said (stating what should have been obvious to Laura but wasn't), since now there was a believable and acceptable public excuse for the separation — namely, Laura's study grant — the faster the dissolution of the marriage could happen, the better for all concerned, especially for Hannah.

Under the weight of Kevin's well-reasoned argument, Laura had backed down. However, the night before Hannah arrived, she had once more begun picking away at the unseemliness of Thanksgiving for such a pernicious announcement. Kevin had shuffled faculty proposals for research grants around on his desk and adjusted his goose-neck lamp so that she was captured in its arc of light. Did she prefer to spoil Hannah's Christmas or her Thanksgiving, he had asked her. He thought his question was valid and its answer clearcut, but Laura felt he was asking the ridiculous — like whether she preferred having her daughter run over by a herd of elephants or by a transport trailer. In the end, as was often the case, Laura had given in, realizing it was useless to argue emotionally with someone who argues rationally.

Kevin had dropped the news on Hannah as soon as Thanksgiving dinner was over — after the turkey and pumpkin pie, but before the soiled dishes were cleared away. Laura had switched on the ceiling light and doused the candles, feeling it was almost sacrilegious to dispense such profane news in the presence of soft candlelight. She had then taken her place at her end of the table, dropped her hands into her lap and begun nervously clicking her butter knife against her wedding ring, waiting for Kevin to utter his life-altering statement. She had watched in gut-wrenching silence as he reached out for Hannah's fingers and curled them around his own, as if he needed some place to anchor his terrible words.

"How could you, Mother!" Hannah had exploded, the moment she had absorbed Kevin's announcement. Her eyes had blazed across her empty plate. "How could you do this?" She had drawn herself up, outraged, tears soundly submerged in her brittle voice. "How could you be so selfish?" Her words had been squeezed together into tight little bunches, and her denouncing tone had said that Laura was the one who was constantly parcelling out life's big and little disappointments to her. Most of all, her tone had implied that it was Laura who was solely and singly responsible for the failure of the marriage.

"You've no right to put us all through this," Hannah had shouted. "You've no right to be so selfish. You just want to get away. The study grant is just an excuse. You just want to leave us."

9

She had ended her outburst by saying, her voice scathing, "For once in your life can't you think of someone besides yourself?"

In those very early moments, Hannah had already been feeling the inconvenience of divided residences, the embarrassment of divorced parents and the pain she and her father were now going to suffer on account of her mother's capricious, selfish whims. Just before she had left the table to take refuge in her room, she had hurled more words directly at Laura.

"It's all so shameful," she had said. "So disgustingly shameful. So shabby. You want to be away from us so you're going to pretend it's on account of your studies." She had ended with a sneer, "You make it sound so noble. So very, very noble."

Whenever Hannah reproves, she does so imperially. Her voice becomes severe and inflexible, reminding Laura of Kevin, who reminds her of her own father. Hannah uses their same intonation, their same "I know I'm right" delivery. Indeed, the three of them — father, husband and daughter, the proverbial three peas in a pod — are so alike that it makes Laura wonder whether genes can only be passed on biologically or whether they can be transmitted by some other process — by osmosis or even by close association with an admired other. Anyway, it has always seemed to her that her husband, who isn't even remotely blood-related to her father, had received more of the MacPhail genes in his make-up than she, the direct issue, had. She often imagined a long line of identical MacPhail personalities going all the way back to Brighton — the ancestral home of her father's father before he had emigrated to Vancouver — all of them carbon copies of each other. But this still didn't explain why Kevin should be so like the MacPhails. His origins were in Manitoba, with a chain of doctors — most of them surgeons in one specialty or another.

Early in Laura and Kevin's relationship — when they had still been able to talk to each other about things more important than whether they could afford to send Hannah to Laval to finish her undergraduate degree, or the high price of cabbage at the Farmer's Market — she had asked Kevin whether he had disappointed his family by choosing to forgo a medical career. He had answered with a laugh, but there had been a twist in his voice that took the lightness from his words.

"I'm a living, breathing, upward-walking disappointment to the whole damn clan," he had said, ramming his hands deep into his pockets like a little boy who knows he is about to be scolded. "Mother was even willing to settle for me being a family practice type of doctor if I'd change my mind about going into academia. She kept pestering me to reconsider my career choice, letting me know they were even willing to accept less from me." He had mimicked his mother's voice — a patient, explaining-type voice: "Everyone doesn't have the makings of a surgeon, you know. But that doesn't mean you can't be a doctor of some sort."

According to Kevin, she'd say this as if everyone had the makings of a doctor of "some sort," but she had always left no doubt that the only real doctors were those who sawed their way through someone's skull or chest, or lopped off someone's arms or legs.

"That's why I ran away to New Brunswick," Kevin had said. "I got as far away as I could." However, he had then quickly amended his words. "Of course, your father was pretty well-known to my supervisor, who said I could do a lot worse than study under MacPhail."

The study grant that Hannah had so imperiously thrown in Laura's face is a year's paid leave — beginning in January — from the high school where Laura teaches English language to students who are developmentally delayed in reading skills. In truth, the grant — which is to be for the study of dyslexia — has absolutely nothing to do with the dissolution of the marriage. It just offers a convenient jumping off point. And, to give Kevin his due, he had carefully pointed this out to Hannah, firmly stating that the marriage was breaking up of its own accord and under its own weight, and that her mother's going away to study was a temporary red herring for the public to chew on until such time as it became convenient to say otherwise. In retrospect, Laura isn't certain whether he had said "convenient" or "expedient." Either way, it

11

didn't matter. At that moment, neither she nor Hannah had been of a mind to make such fine distinctions.

Hannah, completely staggered by the news of the impending marriage break-up, had been interested only in blaming her mother for the family's collapse. And she certainly hadn't been interested in her father's explanation that the dissolution of the marriage was a mutual decision and that the study grant was simply a timely, but innocent, decoy.

T w o

Once Laura reaches the TransCanada Highway, she heads the car up the Saint John River. This early in the day — it is not yet seven o'clock — the highway is practically empty and her tight vigilance is no longer needed. She leans back in her seat and removes one hand at a time from the steering wheel to stretch the cramps out of her fingers. She readjusts the rearview mirror and tilts the sun visor in an effort to settle herself into the seven or so hours of driving ahead of her before she reaches Quebec City. But, just as she finds herself relaxing, just as the tension is leaving her neck, the memory of the past weekend pushes in on her once more, saturating her with its rancid presence, making her realize that it was pure folly to think she could push it aside, even for the length of this trip. Indeed, it has soaked into the nooks and crannies of her vital organs in much the same way as the odour of yesterday's boiled cabbage had soaked into the nooks and crannies of her house.

Recalling the cabbage, Laura smiles thinly. She always has to serve cabbage on Thanksgiving because her father's mother served cabbage on that day. Her father passed the custom on to Kevin, who will pass it on to Hannah, who, in turn, will pass it on to her children. Indeed, Laura thinks that long after she is dead, generations down the line will still have Thanksgiving kitchens filled with the rank and pervasive odour of flaccid cabbage — all because of one old woman's peculiar taste in vegetables.

Laura tries to suppress thoughts of the weekend just past by

13

coaxing other thoughts into her mind. She hops from one happening to another, and settles for a moment on a day last week. It is the day she went to ask her principal for a leave of absence so that she could drive Hannah back to college. Instead of immediately filling out the form that would allow her to bring in the substitute teacher, as he ordinarily would have done, Mr. Stangroom had told her about his recent gallbladder operation, dwelling particularly on the part where his heart had stopped beating and they had had to jumpstart it back to life. He had told her that during those few moments when he had hobnobbed with death, his entire life had passed before him and his sins of omission and commission were outlined, as plain as day, in front of his eyes.

Laura now remembers how she had shamelessly tried to nudge Mr. Stangroom into giving examples of his sins — a nudging, however, that he had easily side-stepped because he was so intent on narrating in minute detail the manner in which his sins had been listed for his viewing. One list, he had said, was headed, "My Life's Regrets," and all of the things he regretted doing and, even more surprisingly, the things he regretted not doing, were garishly displayed on a neon sign that winked and blinked and tantalized like some cheap marquee over a third rate movie house. Working both hands in the air in front of his face, he had pantomimed the rectangular marquee, running his finger down this phantom structure in a one, two, three listing of sins.

Laura also remembers walking back to her classroom that day. She remembers hurrying along the dimly lit corridor that smelled of pubescent sweat and washroom disinfectant, and she remembers her conscious decision to ignore the smell of cigarette smoke coming from the girls' washroom. Not ignoring the smell would have meant a major uproar in her day and immediate expulsion for whoever was sneaking a forbidden drag on a cigarette. In some unexplained way, Mr. Stangroom's revelation had made the infraction of minor school rules suddenly seem unimportant and irrelevant.

As she had hurried along, the signed substitute teacher form clutched firmly in her hand, her mind had been pondering what she would have seen streaming in front of her eyes had *she* been the one on that operating table. She had been particularly interested in the list headed, "Regrets." She had wondered whether great gaudy letters would have proclaimed that she had dropped out of university at the end of her first year — a year that had begun with such fever and promise and had ended in shame, in pregnancy, in marriage. And she had also wondered whether it would have come to the tallyman's attention that, for more than twenty years, she had shared a bed with a man who had never ached for her body with honest lust, and that her early awareness of this — an awareness that was often little more than an uneasy sensation — had torn her own passions to tatters.

Laura glances into her rear-view mirror and catches sight of a van gaining on her, pushing her to move over or pick up speed. Because she is already ten miles over the speed limit, she grudgingly pulls to the right and lets the van go by.

"Bell's Upholstery" is printed on the side of the van in big yellow and black letters. The name "Bell" triggers a long-ago memory and she says "Bell" out loud. She does so partly to bring the memory into focus and partly to break the silence in the car — a silence so thick and charged that it is beginning to suffocate her.

"I used to know a woman named Bell," she says, giving Hannah a quick, slanting glance. "She had the saddest eyes I've ever seen. She was Mother's cleaning lady. I must have been eleven or twelve at the time."

Because Hannah has no intention of being drawn into her mother's makeshift conversation, she offers no response, just shuffles her shoulders ever so slightly, as if the very sound of her mother's voice is an irritant, like the squeak of chalk on a chalkboard.

Not to be put off, Laura continues, "She used to come on Fridays. Bell something or other. I can't even remember her last name."

Once more Hannah shuffles her shoulders and pulls them taut, as if by doing so her body will shield her from the sound of

Laura's voice. Laura notices, but pays no heed and carries on with her story.

"Bell would say the same thing every day. She'd drop down heavily in a chair as if she were a big woman, although she was as thin as a rail. She'd wipe her hands over her face and say, 'Oh, Mrs. MacPhail, the things we do we wish we could undo.' After Bell died, years afterwards, we learned that she had had a child when she was sixteen and her brother and sister-in-law in Prince Edward Island raised him. But they were killed in a car accident when he was twelve. Their car overshot the Cape Tormentine loading wharf. I think that's what happened. Anyway, the boy came to live with Bell, but she could never tell him she was his mother."

Hannah's shoulders hunch even further into her body and Laura finally concedes defeat and stops talking. She waits, breath held in, although she doesn't know what she is waiting for because she certainly doesn't expect Hannah to respond. Eventually, though, the quiet becomes too unsettling even for Hannah, and with exaggerated boredom, and intent only on bringing to a halt what she perceives to be her mother's self-indulgent reminiscing, she sing-songs, "Bell, Bell fell in the well. What the hell! What the hell!"

Afterwards she yawns broadly, as if she is totally jaded from being subjected to such a trite conversation. In a falsely bemused voice, she adds, "Or was it her brother who fell into the Gulf of St. Lawrence. Or was it her kid who fell into the toilet. Now ask me if I care."

Hannah's brazen insolence sends a flash of hot indignation racing through Laura's body. Her neck and hairline begin to feel damp, making her regret not tying her hair back before starting the trip. Heat congregates in her mouth and congeals on her tongue, forming contentious, testy words that she must not let slip past her lips if the next several hours are to be even part way tolerable. To brace herself against being sucked into the black hole of Hannah's anger, Laura digs her fingernails into the steering wheel and sinks them deep into the padded plastic covering.

Although she silently vows to remain mute for the rest of the trip, she feels the need to make one last stab at conversation —

just a sentence or two to explain why she brought up the subject of Bell. She wants Hannah to know that it was not an act of self-indulgence and that she does not have a list of "down memory lane" topics to lay before her daughter while she holds her captive in the car.

She says, tossing her hair back in an off-hand sort of way so that Hannah will know the conversation is only incidental and not leading to anything significant, "The van that just went by a few minutes ago had 'Bell's Upholstery' written on its side. It reminded me of the other Bell. That's the only reason I brought it up. It was just conversation. I was thinking how terrible it must have been for her to carry around a secret like that for a whole lifetime." Although she wants to keep anger out of her voice, a touch of irritation still creeps in, and her words are tinged with the reined-in reprimand she is aching to unleash.

The anger-edged words are not lost on Hannah. Laura knows this from the quick, impatient way Hannah rakes her hand up the side of her head, uselessly pushing back hair that the wind from the open window is tossing about. But still Hannah says nothing. In the silence, Laura hardly dares breathe, hoping that in a second or two her daughter will offer an apology, allowing them to proceed into civil conversation. But after several moments of stony quiet, instead of an apology Hannah flings words out of her mouth — vicious words — and she flings them quickly, as if she's been holding onto them for far too long.

"Speaking of carrying around secrets," she says, racing her words and pitching them over her shoulder so they plunge down hard on the seat between them. "I've had all I can stomach pretending for the past several weeks that I don't know about your little fling at Macquapit Lake. You and that artist fellow." She rolls her mouth into circles as if she's tangling with a hot potato, so that by the time she spits out Claude's name it has a half-witted ring to it: "Clod." She repeats his name several times, each time giving a different pronunciation, each time further exaggerating the roll of her mouth. "Clod. Cloud. Clued. He's the *real* reason for leaving us. But you didn't have the guts to say that. Or maybe it's because you still have some sense of shame left."

If Laura had been punched in the stomach, the oxygen couldn't have left her lungs any faster. She gulps air and buckles forward against the steering wheel. Her breath is sucked inward, making a soft, snagging sound like a sweater sleeve hitching on a bramble bush. The highway in front of her seesaws as she struggles to keep the car under control. She lifts her foot from the gas pedal and eases into the slow lane. Hannah's words eddy around on the sun-warmed leather seat, challenging someone to pick them up. Neither Hannah nor Laura makes a move toward them.

The tension in the car becomes so heavy it takes on a physical presence. The air turns humid, suffocating. To catch her breath, Hannah hurriedly stoops down and rummages in the tote bag huddled at her feet. She pulls out a tape and quickly rams it into the tape deck. It's the tape from *Cats* that Hannah has been playing over and over since early summer, when she saw the musical in London with her grandmother. In a few seconds, music floods the car. Hannah turns her back to Laura again — this time, completely — and begins to hum along with the song, just loud enough to discourage conversation. She wants neither confirmation nor denial from Laura. She wants no conversation on the subject whatsoever. It is too distasteful. For now, it is enough that Laura knows Hannah hasn't been hoodwinked.

Like Hannah, Laura is also strangling on the tension. She opens her window all the way. And, like Hannah, but for a different reason, she also doesn't want to table the subject of Claude for a mother and daughter discussion at this time. Although her meeting with Claude and her impending separation from Kevin are in no way connected, she thinks that yesterday's announcement is still too fresh in Hannah's mind for her to accept this much truth. She understands that if the conversation is broached now, it will only serve to sully Claude's name.

Laura shivers, suddenly feeling chilled even though the sun is streaming in through the open windows. It is as if a raw wind has blown in and has begun ransacking her clothing, searching for seams and buttonholes; it is as if the icy tongue of a winter's day is ravaging her flesh at every entry point. She tries to tug the sleeves of her cotton tee-shirt down over her bare arms. She glances out through her side window, out across the countryside, hoping a glut of fall beauty will warm her flesh. But for all the good the looking does, she might as well be staring at a November landscape — threadbare trees, frozen ground and a sky that is as grey as the pigeons that wobble up and down Queen Street looking for handouts.

She continues driving in the slow lane, and to recapture her composure, she forces herself to concentrate on the music blaring from the tape deck. Mr. Mistoffelees is lamenting that once he was a young and beautiful cat and knew what happiness was, and he wishes for those moments to live again, even if only in memory. His plaintive song reminds Laura that once she, too, had been young — as young as the clever and magical Mr. Mistoffelees.

And she had been beautiful, too. Perhaps not as beautiful as the stripling Mr. Mistoffelees — but she thinks that anyone who fancied the unfrilled, unruffled look of the sixties would have thought her more than passably attractive. Her brown hair was naturally straight, so she didn't have to iron it after every wash, as her girlfriends had to do. And because she had inherited her mother's fine bone structure and her father's green eyes, she could usually pull herself together so you didn't notice that her nose was a trifle too long, her breasts a trifle too small and that her lips needed lipstick to look sensual. Indeed, her lips had rarely looked sensual because she refused to patronize cosmetic companies that tested their products on animals.

Thinking these thoughts, Laura relaxes and begins to smile at the old days, remembering her own days in the sun. She lets her left hand drop from the steering wheel and allows it to rove over her khaki walking shorts, feeling the pinch pleats at the waistband that do such a good job of hiding the slight thickening around her stomach and thighs. She remembers a time when she was so young she hadn't needed any camouflage to hide such imperfections. Ruefully, she recalls how she had taken her springtime body for granted, never once marvelling at the sight of her flat stomach and narrow thighs, and never once realizing that one day those attributes would be hers only through the efforts of aerobic classes and stationary bikes, and by dint of always choosing salads over cheesecakes.

Laura had been barely eighteen when she had entered university. Her sociologist father had been sorely disappointed that the only seed of his loins had opted for literature and refused to make a career in one of the social sciences. Professor MacPhail had always harboured the hope that his daughter would become a second Margaret Mead or Jane Goodall, and to this end he had tried to steer her specifically in the direction of anthropology, stating there was nothing new under the sun in sociology. Laura believed he said this to dim his own disappointment in his sociologist self, having early on given up field research for chalkboards and faculty meetings.

Laura, however, had had her own plans for her life and they did not include researching the mores of distant tribes or cataloguing the mating habits of apes in the wild. She had wanted to be a journalist — a foreign correspondent, reporting news from war ravaged cities in sun-drenched lands. Or, if not a journalist, a writer of novels, like Virginia Woolfe. She had been introduced to *Mrs. Dalloway* in her British Writers course during her second semester at university, and she had practically memorized it.

Now, years later, in the car with Hannah, as she is trying desperately to ignore the words thrown on the seat between them, she can still recall snatches of the story. The incident she remembers most clearly occurs during Clarissa Dalloway's party. Clarissa is wearing a silver-green mermaid's dress — a dress that shows that the years have been good to her body — and she is moving about her living room, mingling. But even as Clarissa makes polite talk with her guests, she is acutely aware that Peter Walsh, her former lover, is watching her from his position beside her fireplace. She feels the intoxication of the moment, feels her heart quivering with exquisite sensations. In turn, these exquisite sensations cause her to remember another time, an earlier time, when she had descended stairs, dressed in white, and had whispered to herself, *"If it were now to die, 'twere now to be most happy."*

As Laura drives along the highway, she forces herself to think thoughts that will block out Hannah's fiercely flung words. She recalls that it was close to twenty-two years after her first reading of *Mrs. Dalloway* that she had experienced her own exquisite moment. It had been in August — the August just past. She had been wearing walking shorts, of much the same colour as the pair she has on today, and a green cotton tee-shirt. She had been at Macquapit Lake, lying on the grass behind her cottage, half-hidden by a bed of flowers. Her eyes had been closed, and she had allowed her bare toes to flirt with the pink and purple blooms of the tall lupins that always seemed to thrive in that part of the meadow. They grew in a helter-skelter way, without pampering or coddling. The sun had been high in the sky — bold and feverish. The stillness of the afternoon had been so drenching that she could hear in the distance the lazy wash of the waves upon the lake shore.

Claude had come searching for her, to tell her he was going back to Montreal. He had stealthily come upon her and stooped down and kissed her full on the mouth. Then, while her lips were still moist from that kiss, he had picked her up in his arms, as effortlessly as if he were picking up his palette, and carried her into her cottage, into her bedroom. He had laid her down on her bed, as carefully and as gently as if he were setting down priceless china. Then he had sat down on the bed beside her and run the back of his slightly cupped hand softly over her cheek, and whispered, "I love your face. I love your sad, beautiful face."

She had known, without his having to say so, that he had never spoken those particular words in that particular tone to anyone else. And certainly no one else had ever spoken them to her. Their freshness had made her breathless. She had felt as lightheaded and as heady as if she had set her foot down on virgin soil, as if she had climbed Mount Everest and erected the first flag at the very top. And minutes later — or was it hours (she couldn't tell because it seemed that time had stretched out beyond the constraints of normal time, stretched out into infinity, into boundless summers and autumns) — she had felt Claude's naked body covering hers. The harsh, institutional-green stucco walls of her bedroom had become soft and hazy and indistinct, like a Monet painting. Her lumpy, "good enough for the cottage" mattress had floated underneath her as if it were filled to overflowing with freshly picked rose petals. And within this bower of love and passion, her flesh had yielded up its hunger, its sadness, its loneliness. And, like Mrs. Dalloway, she had whispered, "*If it were now to die, 'twere now to be most happy.*"

Hannah squirms impatiently in her seat, as if the trip has already taken hours. She reaches over and jacks up the volume on the tape deck. Music fills every nook and cranny in the car. *Midnight, not a sound from the pavement.* Because the melody is so seductive and because Laura's thoughts are so silky and fresh from remembering Claude, she finds herself whispering the words of the song, making sounds under her breath, like a nun alone in chapel praying her Office. Gradually, her voice gets louder and louder. Moments later, she forgets about the words Hannah has flung between them. She forgets about Hannah's sulking. She even forgets about Kevin. Her voice rises full throttle. *Has the moon lost her memory ...*

"Laura!" Hannah hollers, her fury giving her licence to discount their relationship. "Get a grip!"

For Hannah, it is as though all of those years when her mother fell far short of her daughterly expectations have come spiralling together into this one final, confining moment. "For heaven's sake, chill out before someone radios the Mounties! They'll think I stuck a shiv in you, or something."

Hannah notices that Laura is once again pulling back into the fast lane and is rapidly picking up speed. She threatens darkly, "If we get pulled over, I'll say you've gone off your medicine again. I'll say I'm taking you back to the nut-house. I swear I'll do that. I'll embarrass you as much as you'll embarrass me."

Laura pays no heed to her daughter's admonishments. They neither surprise, nor shock, nor sadden her. It is as if she has become inured to them. She has always known that she falls short of the pinnacle of parental perfection that Hannah has chosen to allocate to Kevin. She recalls that even this very morning when she was packing the car in preparation for the trip, she had noticed Hannah giving her a critical once-over look and she knows Hannah was thinking that walking shorts and bare feet in red keds was not suitable attire for a mother taking her daughter back to college. Laura believes that Hannah would have preferred something more sedately frumpy, although, to be quite truthful, she has never been sure what would make her suitable in Hannah's eyes.

In her haste to roll up the window and keep the shame of her mother's shouting inside the car, Hannah snares several strands of her wind-tossed hair between glass and frame. She snaps these free and gives the window handle a final yank before looking around wildly to see if other cars are within hearing distance.

Once the windows are shut tight, Hannah resumes her river-staring position, but her anger is too overwhelming to allow her to sit silently. She jerks around and says, shouting to make certain she'll be heard above the tape deck and above her mother's singing, "Dad wouldn't embarrass me like this. He's so different from you. I don't know why you two ever got married in the first place. Go figure." Without turning her body, Hannah gestures her head toward the spot on the seat where she threw her previous words. As if she is looking into a bucket of slime, she says, "Especially if you wanted to carry on with Clot."

Her anger still not vented, she adds, "I bet Dad doesn't know about Clot. Does he? I think he should know. And he will. Soon."

Laura pauses in her singing long enough to say easily, "No. I don't believe he does know." She quickly picks up the song again, as if she is oblivious to Hannah's threat.

Over the years, Laura has developed a knack for blocking out what she doesn't want to hear and of not seeing what she doesn't want to see. She has always managed to keep every aspect of her life neat and tidy and under control, never letting anything untoward push its way out. Throughout her marriage, she has been convinced that if one untoward thing were to escape, others would surely come rushing out, like water pouring out of a culvert. Sometimes she likens her life to one of those plastic raincoats that are packaged in tiny compact pouches. When the pouch is opened, the raincoat becomes bigger than its package — so big, in fact, that it can never again be stuffed back inside the pouch. Right at this moment, Laura is afraid that if she stops singing, or if she picks up the words on the seat, or if she even acknowledges to Hannah that Kevin wouldn't embarrass his daughter by singing unduly loudly, or that he should, indeed, be told about Claude, the plastic pouch in which she keeps herself encased will burst open and she will tell Hannah why she and Kevin got married. She might even tell her why they had stayed married.

T h r e e

Kevin Stevenson was Professor MacPhail's prize import from Vancouver. Professor MacPhail himself had enticed Kevin to come to New Brunswick, offering him the opportunity to finish his Ph.D. dissertation while doing three-quarter time lecturing in the Sociology Department. It was understood that Kevin would be placed on the tenure track if he proved himself worthy. Since Kevin was from Professor MacPhail's *alma mater* and, like him, was also a Vancouverite, worthiness was a non-issue. A University of British Columbia graduate would certainly be enough of a guarantee in and of himself.

And so it happened that, when Laura was eighteen, she fell in love — or what, at the time, she took to be love. It happened during the first Sunday Kevin came to her house for dinner. She thought his strong jawline and rumpled blondish hair made him look just like Robert Redford, or perhaps Warren Beatty, although she allowed that Warren's hair was a lot darker than Kevin's. Indeed, she was so taken with him that she immediately regretted ignoring her mother's suggestion that she wear the pink silk dress she had bought a few weeks earlier for a family wedding. Instead, she wore a loose peasant-style blouse and even looser elephant pants that hid her long legs — her best body part, she always felt.

In addition to being handsome, Kevin wasn't the usual toadying, obsequious graduate student. And certainly Laura, if anyone, was well qualified to make such observations. She had seen enough of such types come and go. Indeed, it had come to the

25

point where she could predict when a new graduate student would nod his head in assent or shake it in consternation over one of her father's dinner table pronouncements.

Professor MacPhail's pronouncements were *always* predictable, centering around his perception of the limitations of the Maritime universities in comparison with those out West. He usually let the conversation spread out to include the lack of academic scholarship in any given crop of new freshman students. "They get less qualified every year," he would say, his voice case worn. "I don't know how they expect us to do anything with them." To round things off, he would end up with a denunciation of the "Number Crunchers" department, stating that the Administration forgot they were on campus solely to serve the teaching faculties, and not the other way around.

"They haven't the faintest notion of what it takes to run a research-oriented faculty," he would say, and here again his tone would become long-suffering. "No more idea than the man in the moon what it takes to run labs and keep field research underway. All they know about is budget. It's like a god with them. Our research is held up for ransom by the number crunchers."

He would then shake his head wearily, as though his patience had been frayed beyond repair, but even before the first complaint was fully out of his mouth, the new graduate-recruit's forehead would be puckering in empathetic consternation.

Laura noticed immediately that Kevin reacted differently. He listened politely for a short while to her father's complaints — even accepted his advice on how to deal with "the system," saying it was always good to know the inner workings of a place because it prevented useless butting of heads. But she could see that he was just marking time until there was a lull in the conversation and he could take charge of the discussion to direct it to his own interests. She watched as he pushed to the edge of his chair, waiting for a chance to break in with his own agenda, his impatience barely in check. Actually, it was this passion for his field, combined with his lack of fawning deference to her father, that made him so instantly alluring to Laura. It gave him a definite erotic dimension that she had found lacking in the other graduate students.

Laura loved her father dearly and it wasn't because she wanted to see him get his comeuppance at the hands of a graduate student that she took such delight in Kevin's assertiveness. It was simply that no one — including herself, including her mother — had ever taken hold of her father's conversations and subtly deflected them to other issues. The novelty of Kevin's cocksuredness was heady and dizzying.

Over the course of many Sunday dinners, Laura continued to watch Kevin edge forward on his chair, impatient to talk about his own research. His area of interest was the effect of relocation on the inhabitants of a rural community. In fact, it was the opportunity to study the inhabitants of the communities that had been displaced and/or relocated on account of the Mactacquac Dam project on the outskirts of Fredericton that had been the major enticement for his coming to New Brunswick. Of course, Kevin was astute enough to allow Laura's father to think it was the MacPhail powers of persuasion that had brought him there.

Although Kevin came to dinner almost every Sunday, to Laura's dismay he always left immediately after the meal, apologizing for his early leave-taking by saying he had to go back to his dorm and pull some order into his Monday morning eight-thirty lecture. Sunday after Sunday it was the same ritual. By the time October arrived, Kevin had enjoyed months of Sunday dinners, and Laura had come to realize that if she were ever to see him alone, or if he were ever to see her as more than an extension of her parents, it would be up to her to bring it about.

She conscripted the help of her friend Janet to work on what she called "project Kevin," and after a few ideas had been exchanged, they came up with a scheme that was guaranteed fail-proof. On one specific Sunday evening at a prearranged time, Janet was to call and cancel her plans to go with Laura to the late movie. According to the scheme, Laura was to return to the dinner table, dispirited, and announce that she was going to have to go to the movie by herself because Janet had just cancelled.

"Forget about the movie, Laura," her father said, just as they had predicted he would, after she slouched back to the dinner table following Janet's contrived phone call. "I don't want you out that late by yourself." He waved his hands dismissively, a mannerism that always meant the subject was closed.

"But it's the last night for *Bonnie and Clyde*," she wailed, her body sagging in her chair, her disappointment seemingly sincere. "Warren Beatty and Faye Dunaway are in it. Everyone says it's great."

As she had hoped, and according to plan, Kevin came to her deliverance. He hedged ever so slightly — just enough to whet the edge of her apprehension. He then pushed his chair back from the table, crossed and uncrossed his legs and gave a little clearing-of-the-throat type of cough. Then he tilted his head in her father's direction, a petitioning look on his face.

"I've been meaning to see that movie myself, Professor. Laura could come with me. I'd see to it she got home safely." He paused slightly before adding, "And I've got my class material pretty well caught up."

Laura wasn't sure then, or for that matter ever afterwards, whether the deferential tilt of Kevin's head was to request permission to accompany her to the movie, or to ask for a dispensation from reworking his Monday morning lecture. And she also wasn't sure then, or for that matter ever afterwards, whether Kevin truly wanted to accompany her to the movie, or whether he simply wanted to ingratiate himself a little deeper into the good graces of her father. At the time, such details were irrelevant.

The following weekend, Kevin needed no contrived phone call. Just before Mrs. MacPhail brought in the dessert, he asked Laura if she would like to hear a concert that was being held on the campus. This time, a glance at her father was all that he offered in the way of asking for permission. Laura believed that her father gave his immediate delighted consent because he thought his high-spirited daughter could use the settling effect of a mature graduate student. Indeed, he acted as if her twinning with Kevin was already an established fact. He flailed his hands as if he were shooing away pesky flies.

"You kids run along as soon as you're finished. Mother and I'll do the dishes. Won't we, Mother?"

The weekend dates quickly moved to weekday dates. Laura and Kevin met at the student cafeteria between their classes. By the end of a month, it was understood that they had indeed twinned. It took another two months and two days before they became "intimate" — the term Mrs. MacPhail was later to use to describe her daughter's late afternoon conjoinment with her husband's prize graduate student.

"Intimate" was not a term Laura would have used to describe this conjoining. Intimate, as far as she was concerned, elicited thoughts of boudoirs and scented baths and lacy petticoats and secret hideaways and sparkling champagne in crystal glasses. It had absolutely nothing to do with dormitory rooms, soiled sheets and beer bottles in ragged cartons.

The conjoining had come about without premeditation on the part of either of them. Much later in her life, in what she came to think of as the "seasons of her sorrow," it brought her a measure of comfort to know that their late afternoon sexual encounter in Kevin's dormitory had been brought about more by fluke than design. This lent it the randomness of fate and the stuff of Greek tragedies — a style more in keeping with her sensibilities. Of course, she had to admit that fate had been urged on by a pinch of sexual craving and a glass or two too many of warm beer and weak punch.

She and Kevin had accepted an invitation to an afternoon beer bash, hosted by a fellow graduate student who lived off-campus. The beer was plentiful, and Laura, trying to hide her lack of sophistication — everyone in the room was eight to ten years older than she — emptied her bottle time and again as if she were drinking tap water and trying to quench a great thirst.

Although Kevin was also drinking, he saw what was happening to Laura and insisted that they leave the party early, strongly overriding her objections by reminding her that he was driving and wanted to get off the road before it got dark. Because he didn't want to take Laura to her parents' house in her inebriated state, he suggested they go to his place until they both sobered up.

Although there are wide gaps in Laura's memory regarding certain parts of this incident — for instance, when did the moment turn from marking time into a full-blown sexual liaison? — she does remember the two of them walking up the stairs to Kevin's dormitory room, she leaning slackly into him and giggling at something that seemed hilariously funny.

Kevin confessed that his place was a mess, and years later Laura thinks that this confession contained more truth than any other words they spoke to each other for the rest of that afternoon. On some days — her cynical days — she thinks it contained more truth than any other words they spoke to each other for the length of their marriage.

Kevin's dormitory floor was littered with a mix of orange peels that had missed the garbage can and dirty laundry that hadn't made it all the way to the hamper. Beer cans and pop bottles vied for space on his bureau top with crumpled balls of yellow typewriter paper. But more offending than the litter was the obvious lack of privacy. The lock on Kevin's door was broken, and although Kevin assured her that no one would come in without knocking, she kept expecting the students, who were constantly running through the hall and shouting at each other down the full length of the corridor, to barge in.

At her insistence, Kevin wedged a chair underneath the knob of the door, and only after she had tested and retested it did she allow him to manoeuver her to the single bed that was pushed against the far wall. She can still distinctly remember the moment he sidled her down on the unmade bed, one hand easing her onto the narrow lumpy mattress and the other one levelling out the rumpled sheets. However, she has no recollection of any preamble leading up to this tremulous moment. She thinks that there must have been some form of foreplay, possibly even the beginnings of uncontrolled passion, but she wonders how she could forget the passion, yet recall with crystal clarity how Kevin's pillows smelled sour — as if they had been scoured with a mixture of nicotine breath, hair spray and old sweat. And she wonders why she can recall with equal clarity the wall beside his bed that was spotted with bits and pieces of masking tape — curled and yellowed, the remnants of someone else's posters and photographs and girlie calendars.

She also wonders why she remembers that even as Kevin's hands roamed her body, exploring its secrets, she had been thinking that others before her had occupied this same room, this same bed and, without doubt, for this same purpose. Later, she wondered how many other graduate students had made love to how many other virginal girls on that same mattress, and then had moved on, leaving behind them a legacy of stale odours and broken lives. Kevin, to his credit, hadn't moved on, but she sometimes thinks he should have — for both their sakes.

She kept her blouse on while they made love that afternoon, in case the fire alarm went off. Or in case one of the runners in the hall stopped by and the chair didn't hold the door closed. Indeed, if she could have devised a way to carry out the sex act without removing her elephant pants she would have done that too. But since she couldn't, she hung them over a chair at the foot of the bed, where they were close enough that she wouldn't have to forage for them should she have to make a quick exit or find herself in need of a cover-up.

Up until the moment Kevin stripped off his clothes, Laura had never seen a naked male — at least, not one in living flesh. The sight of his raw body battered her senses. Unlike the classical statues, which were all smoothly carved and rounded, Kevin did not look aesthetically beautiful when he was naked. Indeed, she thought he looked spindly and reduced, not nearly as manly and masterful as he had looked in jeans and shirt. She kept staring at his genital area — an area that seemed to her to be strangled in dark underbrush. To divert her eyes from this midpoint, she tried focusing on a line of curly blond hair that climbed up his stomach and curved over his nipples like a Groucho Marx mustache. In different circumstances, she is certain she would have giggled. And, indeed, she thinks she may very well have giggled. It could explain why the sex was such a severe disappointment.

Although Kevin didn't say so, and she surely didn't ask, he appeared to be as inexperienced as herself. What she distinctly remembers of the moment is the two of them thrashing about on the bed as if they were novice swimmers thrown overboard, each one desperately reaching for the lifeline that would save them from drowning. And she also distinctly remembers that, in the midst of this awkward tangle of limbs on the lumpy mattress, they both made urgent promises of love to each other — promises that seemed appropriate at the time, and which she supposes they both meant.

The second time they made sexual contact, the lovemaking was more leisurely. It was in Laura's own home, in her own bed. Her parents had gone to Orono, Maine, on a trip that was part business, part pleasure. Professor MacPhail was meeting a colleague at the University of Maine with whom he was co-authoring a book comparing the French in Northern New Brunswick to the French in Northern Maine. Mrs. MacPhail had persuaded her husband to take her along, so that once the business had been looked after, they could swing down to Portland for a Saturday afternoon shopping spree.

With the house to themselves and the phone off the hook, there was time for Laura to be surprised at how cool Kevin's bare flesh felt against her own naked breasts. And there was time to notice how he carefully balanced himself on his elbows so that she wouldn't have to bear the full weight of his body as they made love — this, though, only after she gasped for air against his chest. And there was time for her to be sad because never once during the whole act did she suck in her breath with unbridled passion — an experience her friends had told her had happened to them.

There were other sexual encounters, mostly furtive. Afterwards — whenever there was time for an afterwards — their conversations lapped around work and plans for the future. When Laura was well into the marriage, it struck her as odd that she hadn't noticed — and she was sure Kevin hadn't either — that during all of those post-coital conversations, her future and his future were not at all congruent. He dreamed about having a faculty position in a prestigious university that was heavily oriented towards social science research. And he dreamed about delivering conference papers at other prestigious universities.

She dreamed about reporting world-altering news from places she only dimly knew existed — places that had sprung into public awareness overnight, mainly because of her on-the-spot reporting of the coup, the uprising, the earthquake or flood. She imagined herself meticulously filing her reports while under siege in these foreign lands, bullets gouging the naked sun-baked ground on which she stood and sending up clouds of dust mere meters behind her back. She imagined herself, seconds after the report was filed, running back to the safety of her hotel to wash the grime from her face and to grab a few minutes of exhausted sleep before going before the cameras again.

Later into the marriage it also struck her as odd that she and Kevin had continued to maintain their budding relationship, even though the sex remained clumsy. However, both Laura and Kevin knew — and knew without ever giving voice to this knowledge — that their relationship pleased Laura's father, and if she and Kevin had anything in common it was this pleasing of her father. As Kevin had become more enmeshed in his studies, he had also become more aware of the influence her father held, not only in his department, but within his faculty — indeed, within the whole university. And Kevin had come to realize that Professor MacPhail's renown as a soundly academic sociologist had spread to other universities. Although, at the time, Laura occasionally surmised that it was this awareness that kept Kevin glued to her, she preferred to think it was the other days — the days when she wasn't MacPhail's daughter and he wasn't MacPhail's doctoral student — that were responsible for cementing each to the other.

Laura resettles herself in her seat, changes her grip on the steering wheel and gives a half-sigh as she recalls one such cementing day in late fall when she and Kevin had walked hand in hand through Odell Park. The warmth of Kevin's flesh had seeped into hers as they had strolled along the path, kicking mounds of dead leaves ahead of them. From time to time she had stooped down to collect a few good maple leaf specimens to take home and coat with glycerine to keep for memories.

She now halts her remembering to frown quizzically, wondering if she still has those leaves packed away in the box with the corsage from her high school graduation, Hannah's christening dress, the newspaper clipping of Mr. LeBlanc's funeral notice, and the white field daisy from Mary/Joseph's grave. She decides she does have them, and returns to her memories to recall that it had been on that same day, during that same walk, that Kevin had said he envied her her uncomplicated life. There had been a story in his voice when he said that, but in her youth and self-absorbtion she had skipped over it as easily as she had skipped over the leaves.

Often, when tragedy strikes and the reality of it is too terrible to absorb, the mind rushes to protect the body by flooding the senses with minute details of one's immediate environment. Little things of the moment stand out in relief, stand out far beyond their ordinary planes. Colours are sharper. Contrasts are greater. Lines are deeper. This is exactly what Laura remembers experiencing during that snowy evening in early March when she told Kevin she was pregnant.

They were sitting in his car, parked in the driveway of her parents' house, having just come back from a movie, *The Graduate*. It was a mild night for the time of year and soft snow was falling. Big fluffy snowflakes were drifting down on the windshield and searching for a purchase on the slippery glass. She and Kevin were talking about the movie — actually Kevin was doing all of the talking — discussing whether Anne Bancroft was a villian or a victim. Laura was absently watching snowflake after snowflake piling up on the windshield, one upon the other in a random and uneven fashion, forming a series of dips and valleys and mountains. At irregular intervals, Kevin would switch on the wipers and the built-up snow would disappear, only to start building up all over again.

From time to time, Laura peered out over the dips and valleys and mountains that the snowflakes were making. From where she sat, she could see in through the large picture window of her parents' living room. She could see her father putting new logs in the fireplace and her mother serving coffee and cake to a couple of faculty friends who were seated on the white brocade couch that was always kept covered with an afghan except when company was expected. The fire from the fireplace was reflected in the windshield of the car, giving a surreal quality to the night, as if another world, an uncomplicated world, existed — a world apart from the one in the car, apart from the one in her parents' house. It reminded Laura of Alice in *Through the Looking Glass* and she wished she just could walk through the snow-piled windshield and into that make-believe world.

Kevin, oblivious to her agitation, rambled on about the movie. Finally, just moments after he had kissed her goodnight — a hurried kiss — saying he wasn't interested in going into her house because he wasn't in the mood to meet company, especially academic company, she blurted out her news.

"I'm pregnant," she said wearily, her strength sapped from having harboured this secret for the past seven days. She wished she were already in bed asleep or that it was tomorrow morning and she had just wakened up from a bad dream.

As soon as the word "pregnant" slipped over her lips, Kevin immediately jerked backwards in his seat as if she had touched his bare skin with a hot wire. "What? What?" he said, pushing the air back with his hands, as if to beat off the terrible word.

She repeated tonelessly, "I'm pregnant. About two months."

Laura's hands had begun to sweat profusely, even though several minutes earlier Kevin had turned off the ignition to save gas and it had quickly become cold inside the car. Her insides trembled. She watched as the windshield piled up with snow again. And she waited for Kevin to say something comforting, but she didn't know what that could be. Finally, when he did speak, he said the words that over the centuries other trapped and terror-filled men have said to other trapped and terror-filled women: "Are you sure? Are you really sure?"

Even in the poor light, Laura could see that Kevin's face was as white as the snow that was still piling up on the windshield. She could smell his fear. It filled the car, eating up the oxygen, leaving the odour of rust behind, like too many plants in a room — a damp greenhouse sort of smell.

Her own fear made her mouth so dry she had to spit out her words as if she were spitting out grit, a morsel at a time. "I'm sure," she said, "I'm very sure." To forestall him from asking yet again whether she was sure, she added, "I went to the Campus Health Services. It's certain. I'm two months."

Kevin lowered his head into his hands in the manner of a man submitting to the guillotine. "No! God, no!" he moaned. "Of all things, not this."

But then, quickly, in his typically expeditious style — a style that had found so much favour with her father — as if he couldn't allow one more moment to pass without getting this problem out of the way, Kevin raised his head and looked directly at her, his hands still cupped and outstretched as if in supplication, his voice shaking. "Abortion. You'll have to get one. Right away!"

It was more of a question than a statement, and when Laura was slow in replying Kevin's voice became fidgetty, hasty for an answer. "I'll ... We'll ... I'll ... We must ... We'll find..." he said, groping for a solution. "It's the only thing."

She wished he would reach out and put his arms around her to comfort her, but instead he circled them around his own body as if he was in greater need of solace himself. She could feel her stomach coiling into a tight little ball, as if it were a small animal protecting itself from a savage blow. Once more, her voice leaked out of her mouth, thin and puny and pinched.

"I won't have an abortion." Her words almost wobbled out of her mouth. She could see her breath suspended between the two of them like a barrier separating one from the other. By now, because clearing the windshield was the furthest thing from Kevin's mind, the snow had piled up so high that she could no longer see the reflection of the fire in her parents' living room. She felt cut off, abandoned. She was certain that no matter what came her way in the future, she would never again experience a moment of such total isolation and desolation.

"Why not, Laura? For God's sake, why not get an abortion?" Kevin asked, his voice reaching her, no longer trembling but harsh-edged, as if he were already exasperated from trying to make her see reason. "We're not ready for this. Not me. Not you. It's the only commonsense thing."

She wished he would shut up talking reason and common sense. She rubbed her hand across her stomach, possessively. "I won't have an abortion," she said stubbornly. "First, when they told me I was pregnant, I prayed for a miscarriage. I prayed right there in the doctor's office. I was even tempted to ask about an abortion. I just wanted to be rid of it. But not long afterwards — I believe it happened even before I left the clinic — I began to feel it was a baby and I knew I couldn't do away with it. No matter what anyone thinks is best."

Again Kevin moaned, "Oh God, no!" and once more his head went back into his hands and he rocked back and forth, comforting himself like a neglected child in a crib. In a few seconds, as if strengthened by the rocking, he faced her down, his voice even more demanding than before. "It's the only way out! It's only a blob at this stage. Can't you see that! So why can't you do it?"

Because earlier Laura had been thinking about Alice in *Through the Looking Glass*, and because she had no answer that would satisfy Kevin, she parrotted softly, as if she were crooning to a child, *"The little fish's answer was, we cannot do it, Sir, because."*

Laura's apparent flippancy in their moment of catastrophe incensed Kevin. "Don't go stupid on me, Laura," he snapped. "The quality of the rest of our lives is at stake." He began to list what was at stake: "My career! Your father is on my external committee. He can really screw me if he wants to. Really jerk me around." He dropped his head back into his hands, forgetting for the moment about the rest of the items on the list, as if his knowledge of the magnitude of the jerking around was too heavy to be held in his head without support.

"And there are more reasons. All kinds of reasons. All kinds. Oh God, what a mess! What a bloody mess!"

Right then, even through her own fear, even through her own upheaval, Kevin looked so pathetic, so wretched, that Laura wished she could say she would get an abortion. Instead, though, she just mumbled, over and over again, "I'm sorry. I'm sorry," not knowing whether she was sorry for the mess of his life or the mess of her own.

Because there was nothing else to say, they both lapsed into silence, each of them contemplating the impending destruction of their lives. Kevin was the first to speak, repeating what he had said before, that an abortion was the only solution.

"I don't love you enough for marriage, Laura," he said with brutal honesty, and then, as if to soften the blow, he added, "And I don't think you love me enough either. We hardly know each other. Just weeks. Mere weeks." He said this, freely abridging the nearly six months they had known each other to suit the circumstances of the moment. "The only option is an abortion. It's the best thing for both our sakes." He then asked, his voice softly entreating, as if she had already capitulated, "You do see that, don't you?"

Just an hour or so earlier, had anyone asked Laura whether Kevin loved her, she would have had no hesitation in saying that certainly he did. And she would have had no hesitation in saying she loved him. She remembered how, a few days earlier, they had built a snowman out of freshly fallen snow and how easily they had laughed when she had said it looked exactly like Réné Levesque, the Parti Quebecois leader. They both had agreed that the only change needed was a cigarette in his mouth instead of a pipe.

"Abortion is out of the question," Laura now said tremulously, her voice betraying the deadness of her own soul. She had always thought that when love left, it did so slowly, petering out over days and weeks, not disappearing in mere moments, as it was now in the front seat of a car with the cold from the leather seat seeping into her kidneys. Because she understood that Kevin related better to reason than to emotion, she explained further, "How do you think I could get an abortion even if I wanted to? I'd have to go to the United States." She gave a slightly ironic laugh.

"You know as well as I do that I can't even go to a late movie by myself, much less take off for Maine for several days. Mom and Dad would have to be told. And they'd never agree to an abortion. Not in a million years."

It was as though in the silent moments, Kevin, too, had seen the impossibility of an abortion. He relented, an undercurrent of understanding creeping back into his voice. "I know. I know." He then added, flatly, with resignation, the pain of lost dreams weighing down each word, "I guess we'll have to get married. It's what your parents will expect. It's the only thing we can do."

"Yes," she echoed, so softly she could barely hear herself. "It's the only thing we can do."

On the day of Laura's wedding, the only patch of pure white in her parents' living room — the nuptial room — was a Bavarian lace cloth on the circular dining room table that had been moved in to hold the food. But even this bit of white was almost invisible under everything that had to be placed on the table in order to feed the forty-five "close-friends" whom Mrs. MacPhail had invited to the wedding. And, of course, the decorations had to be accommodated. For a centerpiece, Mrs. MacPhail had arranged a lead crystal vase overflowing with carnations, each bloom dyed either canary yellow or Mediterranean blue, in keeping with the yellow-and-blue motif Laura had half-heartedly chosen after she had been coaxed and cajoled by her mother into putting the best possible face on things.

Paper napkins — blue nondescript flowers on a yellow background — were humped in a tidy mound beside the freshly-polished silverware. Mrs. MacPhail, with her penchant for detail, had wanted violets on the napkins — violets were the New Brunswick provincial flower — but because of short notice for the wedding, she had settled for flora of no known genus. Actually, she considered herself fortunate to have been able to find the right shade of blue; the yellow was a little off compared to the other yellow decorations. Still, all forty-five napkins were from the same dye lot.

Kevin and Laura's names had been inscribed in the corner of

each napkin, the letters embossed in Mediterranean blue. The raised print stood out, bold and shiny. The only hitch was that, in the folding, the "and" linking the two names and the "L" beginning Laura's had become lost in a crease so that the two names read as one word: "Kevinaura."

The wedding morning was cold and raw — the type of April morning that often shows up in New Brunswick on the heels of an especially hard March. Ice had come down the Saint John River and bunched up in unequal amounts between the two bridges that join Fredericton North to Fredericton South. A city-sponsored lottery was accepting predictions as to when the ice would leave the river, and everyone was saying that at the rate the rain had been falling for the past several days, the break would come sooner rather than later.

Shortly before noon, Mary Ellen, a member of the Faculty Wives Club who was helping Vera with the wedding arrangements, called out across Vera's kitchen, "Vera, how does that saying go about rain on the day of a wedding? Is it 'Happy is the bride the rain rains on.' Or is it the other way around?"

Vera, who was bustling around, certain she would never get everything done in time for the three o'clock ceremony, hastily covered a plate of appetizers with waxed paper and answered impatiently, "Oh, I never pay much attention to that foolishness. Seems to me you can change it to suit yourself."

She gave a quick glance at the small window above her kitchen sink and at the cold water running in sheets down the outside panes. Then she looked into the dining room and saw Laura standing by the table, fiddling with the napkins. She said, more emphatically, "But I think it's 'Happy is the bride the rain rains on.' Yes, I'm sure that's the way it goes."

Laura pretended not to have heard. She was busily rearranging the napkins so that her name wouldn't be partially devoured by the fold. Although it was important to her that her name only be merged — not submerged — she felt so tired and so woebegone that she wondered whether the refolding of all forty-five napkins would be worth the effort.

Even from the distance of the next room, Vera saw her daughter's weariness. She quickly put the airtight plastic-wrapped plate of sandwiches in the refrigerator and then went into the dining room to insist that Laura get some rest. She shushed Laura off to her bedroom with the admonishment that it was more important for her to look rested for her wedding that afternoon than to bother with refolding the napkins.

Laura put up no resistance. She felt dead tired. And she knew why. She hadn't slept the night before, on account of a silly dream. She had gone to bed early, again at her mother's suggestion, but she had lain awake, her eyes scanning her girlish bedroom that in less than twenty-four hours would no longer be solely hers, but would have to be shared with Kevin whenever they visited her parents. Even in the dark she could pick out her possessions — stuffed animals, ribbons won on the debating team and the swimming team, a collage of photographs containing her favourite teachers as well as her best friends, and a picture of her cat, Wimpy, who had been so pampered it had taken old age to bring him to his grave. Her mind's eye had also taken in the Victorian wallpaper and the frilly curtains that were an uncanny match for her mother's Royal Albert china pattern, Lavender Rose. Just before she had fallen asleep, she had remembered how she had fought and lost the battle to have her walls painted in psychedelic colours — like her friend Janet's room, like almost every teenager's room in the mid-sixties. And she had wanted a black light. But her mother wouldn't even let her wear tie-dyed shirts. She said they were too hippy.

She had no sooner drifted into sleep than the dream had begun. She had dreamt that she and Kevin were standing on the corner of Queen and York, just across from City Hall. Kevin was wearing a raincoat and she was decked out in full bridal regalia — veil, train, bouquet, blue garter. She had even adhered to an old family custom and placed a penny in her shoe to ward off poverty. People on their way to work had bunched up on the sidewalk and were shouldering each other out of the way to get a better look at the bride and groom. Reverend Bradscome, who had been engaged by Mrs. MacPhail to officiate at the wedding, and who, like the flowers on the napkins, had been settled for on account of the short notice, was standing at a lectern waiting for them to come forward. He also was wearing a raincoat, the tail of which was billowing out in the wind like a grand lady's bustle.

"My brothers and sisters," he intoned, as he crouched over the lectern like a hawk over carrion, "we are gathered here this morning to determine the suitability and perfect oneness of Kevin Stevenson and Laura MacPhail for holy matrimony."

To prove this suitability and perfect oneness, Kevin and Laura were to repeat verbatim whatever Reverend Bradscome read from an old newspaper that moments earlier he had picked out of the gutter and placed on the lectern. As he rubbed his hand across the crumpled, yellow pages he stressed that he wanted nothing less than verbatim repetition. From somewhere in the direction of City Hall a choir echoed, "Verbatim! Verbatim! Verbatim!"

As soon as he was ready to get the ceremony underway, Reverend Bradscome caught Laura's eye and nodded, indicating that it was her turn to come forward. Nervously, she clutched a fistful of white satin and, careful to keep the hem of her dress from dusting the street, picked her way through the crowd.

"To think I'd see Bengal before I'd die," Reverend Bradscome said, reading slowly and clearly, as if he were talking to a person with a hearing impediment.

As soon as he finished, Laura stepped to the lectern and parroted his words exactly. The crowd applauded as she walked back down.

Reverend Bradscome then beckoned Kevin to come forward. Although, by this time, outside of her dream, Laura's carnal passions for Kevin had withered to a mere trickle, inside her dream she still felt a shiver of delight, as handsome, tall-above-the-crowd Kevin pushed his way forward, assured and confident.

"To think *I'd die* before *I'd see* Bengal," he read, his voice ringing out loud and clear in the crisp morning air.

Laura immediately caught the error and gasped audibly. Wildly, she darted a look over the crowd to see if anyone else had noticed that he had transposed the words. When she saw that the crowd's attention had been momentarily captured by a very large and ornate thurible which was billowing out heavy grey incense, she tried frantically to signal to Kevin. She mouthed silent words, working her lips furiously, righting the arrangement of the sentence. Kevin, oblivious to his mistake, looked at her with annoyance, as if she were trying to steal his moment. Even Reverend Bradscome didn't notice the error because seconds later he pronounced them husband and wife. Thunderous applause followed, everyone confirming the oneness of the bride and groom, everyone confirming their marriage suitability. Laura's body went weak with gratitude that they had gotten away with the deception.

Upon awakening, Laura had tried to shake off the dream. But it continued to nag at her. She analyzed it. Dissected it. Probed it. She chastised herself for wasting precious sleep on account of such stupidity, and asked herself over and over why she was putting so much stock in a silly dream. Just because the marriage hadn't been planned — or, for that matter, intended — there was no reason to believe they wouldn't make suitable marriage partners. She was convinced that, for the sake of the child, if they put their minds to it — *really* put their minds to it — she and Kevin could become suitable partners. She acknowledged that the magic had evaporated. Like the Cheshire Cat, it had faded away quite slowly, beginning with the end of the tail and ending with the grin — so much so that, right now, not even a reflection of the grin remained. It had spent itself in paper napkins and dyed flowers and in disillusionment and aborted dreams. But from all she had heard, even under the best of circumstances passion had a short shelf life, and she was certain her marriage would be able to survive quite well without such temporal dizziness. For the child's sake, she and Kevin would manufacture a marriage based on truth, loyalty and respect. If dizziness came, she would be grateful for the bonus.

She reminded herself that her father and mother believed that she and Kevin were suited to each other — or at least suited enough considering the circumstances. And there was no doubt that Kevin was well suited to them, although she was aware that they would have preferred him to have postponed the marriage bed consummation long enough to permit them a more traditional wedding for their only daughter — at least traditional enough to prevent them from having to fabricate stories to explain its hastiness.

The moment that Laura had broken the news to her father that she was going to be marrying Kevin, she felt that he forgave her for not going into the social sciences. Having a son-in-law in the field, especially one with such promise, would be sufficient to carry forward the family honours. However, when she had added the mitigating circumstance — that she was pregnant — his voice had instantly changed its tone. "My God! My God! Don't tell me that!" he had burst out, with a protesting wail reminiscent of Kevin's.

Laura told her father the news during breakfast. He had stared at her for several seconds, a ghastly look on his face as he held a quivering spoonful of granola partway to his mouth. Then, as if his hand had suddenly gone numb, he had dropped his spoon into his cereal bowl, so that milk and soggy granola splashed over the black-and-white placemats that matched, check for check, the squares of tile on the floor.

"Mom, I'm pregnant," Laura had said to her mother earlier that morning, while Vera MacPhail was portioning out her husband's granola — enough to give him energy, not enough to inflate his cholesterol. Donald MacPhail was in the bathroom taking a shower. Vera had gasped and grabbed at her heart. "Oh no. Oh Lord, no!" She had shot a look towards the bathroom and moaned, "Poor Donald. Poor Donald." Laura was forever grateful that at least she hadn't said, "Are you sure. Are you really sure?"

But as soon as Vera had absorbed the fact of the pregnancy, she lashed out at the scandalous nature of Laura's imprudent behaviour. Vera, a woman not ordinarily given to shouting, had shouted, although she was careful to shut the kitchen door so as not to alarm Donald. "Are you telling me you became intimate with a man, weeks, not even months, after you started going with him!" The muscles in her jaw had tightened and loosened as she repeated over and over again, horror-struck, "You barely knew the boy."

It seemed to Laura that the fact of her out-of-wedlock pregnancy was only slightly more terrible to her mother than her precipitous bedding — her willing, and untimely to the point of bad taste, deflowering. She wondered whether her mother would have taken the news any better if she had been told that the deflowering had been carried out under the influence of warm beer and tepid punch.

Because Laura had told her mother the news first, Vera MacPhail had had time to gain a small amount of composure. Once Laura had broken the news to her father, Vera had rushed over to Donald, wanting only to calm him down.

"Don't, Donald! Don't, dear!" she had cautioned. "Don't get excited! Your blood pressure! Remember your blood pressure!"

"Is she sure?" he had asked in a tremulous voice, looking in Laura's direction. "Is she really sure?" Vera had nodded and, in her desperation to pacify her husband, had unintentionally whittled away at the last shreds of Laura's self esteem and, for all intents and purposes, held the rest of her life up for ransom.

"She's sure, dear. And he did consent to marry her. So many other young men would have made her go it alone. We must always be grateful to Kevin for that, dear." She had added, and this was for Laura's benefit, "Even if by her imprudent behaviour," and she had pronounced "imprudent" solidly and with satisfaction, as if she were stomping a bug under her shoe, "she has ruined her chances for a university education and sullied her good name." Although it was left in silent parentheses, Laura knew that her mother had been saying that she had ruined the good name of her parents as well.

Vera and Donald MacPhail were not the sort of parents to sire a daughter who would get caught up in a hasty marriage, nor were they the type to have a son-in-law to whom they would have to be grateful for taking their despoiled daughter off their hands. Vera, in particular, was mightily shaken by the shotgun nuptials. She had always lived her life according to temperance, order and convention, and had expected no less from flesh of her flesh, bone of her bone.

She, herself, had waited for marriage until she was thirty-eight — although in truth she hadn't waited all of those years for marriage. She had waited all of those years for Donald.

When she had finished her commercial course at seventeen, she had landed a job in the steno pool of the university's Humanities faculty. Five years later, Donald had been brought in from Vancouver to take over as Chairman of the Sociology Department. He had needed an administrative assistant and he had chosen Vera over thirty-seven other applicants. That first morning, when Vera went into Donald's office to pick up his outgoing mail, she had fallen instantly and intensely in love with him. She was twenty-two at the time.

Throughout Laura's teenage years, during any and all mother-daughter conversations having to do with love, lust and sex — such conversations having been uncomfortably initiated by Vera MacPhail for the protection of Laura's virtue — Vera was always quick to say that never once during the almost fourteen passion-parched years that she had waited for marriage to Donald did she permit herself by word or deed to betray her erotic feelings towards him.

She would say, as though it shouldn't need saying, that Donald was a married man at the time and she was no temptress. She would always purse her lips and incline her head towards the university as if to say that she could give Chapter and Verse to temptresses at that place. And she could name male professors — married ones — who had let their sideburns grow long and had taken to wearing turtleneck sweaters to make them appear younger so they could dally with their female students. Once, she had even hinted that she knew of a few male professors who had dallied with their male students.

In defense of her virtue — virtue that she expected Laura to emulate — she would always point with pride to her discretion in all of her dealings with Donald: Never once had she brushed against his hand deliberately. Never once had she consciously grazed his shoulder with her own. Not even fleetingly. And unlike those other secretaries who flirted so disgustingly with their professor bosses, she hadn't even allowed herself to hold Donald's gaze a moment longer than was necessary for business-essential communication.

During the course of these conversations, however, Laura would notice that her mother's voice would harden and the creases down the sides of her mouth would deepen — just as if she were still begrudging those years of virtuous restraint — restraint that would have continued if the first Mrs. Donald hadn't paved the way for the second Mrs. Donald by dying peacefully after a short illness.

Immediately after her marriage to Donald — just eleven months after the demise of the first Mrs. Donald — Vera gave up her office work in favour of homemaking and involvement in community organizations. Nine months and three days into the marriage she produced her one and only offspring. Laura had often thought that it was lucky for her mother's reputation that her daughter had been tenacious enough to cling onto the womb for the full term, plus a few buffer days.

Even though Donald and Vera were acutely ashamed of their daughter's hurried-up marriage, they still managed to put the best possible face on it. Kevin's two-year contract with Dalhousie University in Nova Scotia — a contract which began with intersession and summer school — was the reason they gave for the rushed nuptials.

On several occasions, within Laura's hearing, Vera had confessed to friends — always with a little flutter of her hand, always with a casual toss of her head — that certainly she was disappointed she hadn't been given time to put on a proper wedding. She would always quickly dismiss her disappointment, though, saying it wasn't her feelings that were at stake.

"Young couples today are not like we were," she would say, her voice holding just the right mix of thwarted expectations and reined-in pride. "They won't settle for being parted until a time becomes more convenient."

She would then invoke Kevin's name with a proprietary air. "Besides, our Kevin has just landed himself an enviable teaching contract at Dalhousie. A great beginning for a brand new Ph.D."

Of course, she would neglect to say that Donald had pulled in all of his markers, and whatever other favours he had outstanding, in order to get the expectant couple out of town. As she talked, Mrs. MacPhail would fiddle with invisible pleats in her fine wool skirt while her mind raced ahead, hoping that the two-year contract would blur the less than nine months gestation period of her first grandchild.

In later years, especially after the birth of Hannah, Laura was better able to understand Vera's acute disappointment with her daughter's rushed marriage and with the bare-armed, street-length wedding dress that went along with it. Vera had dreamed of seeing her daughter walk down the aisle of St. Anne's Anglican Church in full bridal attire. Now, this dream had to be cast aside. "Anything more elaborate would be seen to be in bad taste should things ever surface," was the way Vera put it. But it was a dream that had died hard because Vera herself had forgone a white wedding — again, of course, in the interest of good taste, Donald being so recently widowed.

During her growing up years, Laura had often looked at her mother's wedding photos. She had seen a tightly girdled middle-aged woman in a green gabardine suit. A little brown velvet hat, with a dyed-to-match feather sidling up its brim, was perched sedately on her head and hid the tightly permed hair that only poked out in a few places around her cheeks. Her medium-heeled pumps looked solid, but certainly not bridelike. Indeed, Laura often thought that her mother looked no different on her wedding day than she did on other days of the week when she went shopping or to church, or off to the many organizations which collected funds for various and sundry body parts — heart, lungs, bone marrow. Looking at the photos had always made Laura feel sad, as if her mother had suffered a great deprivation, and she had vowed that when her time came for marriage she would make it up to Vera by being bridal-looking enough for both of them. However, her loose-waisted, sleeveless, beige linen dress fell far short of being bridal enough for one person, let alone for two.

This was probably why, when Hannah was born, all constraint was thrown aside for her christening dress. It had yards and yards of lace, and mounds of white satin. It was a dress that could be considered overdone for royalty, much less the grandchild of Vera and Donald. It was as though Laura and her mother, in silent complicity, had decided it was high time for one of the Stevenson women to wear white fluff through a rite of passage.

F o u r

"Can't we stop soon? I'm sick and tired of being in the car," Hannah asks Laura, her tone petulant. She looks out through the car window to see how far they've come. She makes it sound as if she's been asking to stop for hours without getting a response. "I'm hungry and I want to use the bathroom."

Hannah's wailing reminds Laura of the family's several car trips to see her parents in Vancouver after her father accepted early retirement and moved back to the family homestead. Hannah would begin her pestering questions almost before they left the driveway in Fredericton.

"Are we almost there? I'm tired of the car," she would say, squirming fussily and throwing her small, furry toys on the floor as though they were the cause of her discomfort.

Kevin's tolerance never wavered, but Laura remembers that her own patience was always short-lived and she would end up snapping that she could do nothing to make the distance any shorter. But, although the snapping was directed at Hannah, it was really meant for Kevin. If he hadn't been so stingy with his time they could have taken three weeks' vacation instead of two. There could have been more breaks along the way and the trip wouldn't be so tiring. She knew that Kevin even begrudged taking those two weeks away from his research, but he believed strongly that Hannah should know her grandparents.

Often Kevin would try to ease the tension on the drive by assuring Hannah that the next trip out West would be in an airplane, although he knew, as well as Laura did, that they would never be able to afford air fare for the three of them, and that the next trip and the next trip and the trip after that would be in their small economy-size car, in the heat of summer, and always under the constraints of time. But he knew it sounded good to Hannah. And he always placated Hannah by suggesting, as Hannah surely knew he would, that she come up in the front seat and sit between him and Laura. For the next several miles, the three of them would sit squeezed together, hot and uncomfortable, until finally Laura would give in to the overcrowding and elect to sit alone in the back seat.

Neither Kevin nor Hannah ever seemed to notice Laura's sacrificial exile. They just kept chatting to each other, Hannah quickly forgetting that she had ever been bored. Laura's hurt would simmer all day, and by nightfall when they reached their hotel, her temper would explode over some trivial inconvenience — the water in the shower not being hot enough, a burnt out light bulb, towels too few or too skimpy. Kevin and Hannah would exchange looks, as much as to say, "I don't know what brought this on."

Always, after these outbursts, Laura would be mortally ashamed of herself, ashamed of wilfully coveting the time Hannah spent with Kevin. She believed her stinginess made her an unnatural mother, and to compensate for this aberration she would give Hannah extra hugs and kisses when she put her to bed and special treats when she didn't even deserve them. However, much as an animal senses that a predator is near, Hannah instinctively sensed that her mother's affection was begrudged, and she always accepted the hugs and kisses with a practiced wariness.

"Don't do that, Mom," she would reproach, wiping her mother's kiss away with her chubby little hands. "Your lips are wet. You make my face all slobbery."

Laura straightens up in her seat and leans forward over the steering wheel to get a better look at her surroundings. The Saint John River has disappeared, and in its place there are only potato fields and more potato fields.

She responds to Hannah's peevish request to stop by pointing up the road. "If my memory serves me correctly," she says, trying to bring into memory her other journeys over this section of highway, "there's a service station up ahead. With a diner. Irving. Or Texaco. Or Shell. Or whatever." To let Hannah know that she isn't being inconvenienced by stopping, she glances at the fuel indicator on the dashboard and says easily, "And this is as good a place as any to tank up. I'm getting low on gas."

"I'm not going in if the place is a dump," Hannah says, as if she is still spoiling for a fight. "I don't want one of those places where you have to ask for a key — where you have to make a public announcement that you want to use the toilet."

Even before Hannah is finished speaking, they round a curve and the service station comes into sight.

"There it is!" they say in unison, both pointing to the left side of the highway about a quarter of a mile away.

When they come abreast of the diner, Laura slows down and pulls off the highway. Hannah, anxious to make a fast exit, quickly shoves her bare feet into her running shoes and grabs her tote bag, reshuffling the stuff that is spilling out of its mouth, and positioning herself to bolt for the door. The instant the car stops, Hannah gets out and rushes on ahead. Laura takes her time and fills up the gas tank, allowing Hannah plenty of lead room in case the place isn't up to her standards.

The diner is scruffier than Laura remembers, but she knows it must have met Hannah's lower-end standards of acceptability or she wouldn't have gone into the bathroom. The place has a one-colour decor — a heavy mustard yellow, the colour raw egg yolks turn after they've been exposed too long to the air. Because it is late for breakfast and early for lunch, the diner is almost empty. Laura takes a booth at the far end of the room, where she can see Hannah when she comes out of the bathroom.

As soon as Laura slides into the seat, the waitress, who is dressed in the same mustard yellow as the vinyl on the booths, brings over a thermos of coffee and tells her that her daughter has already placed an order for fries and a Coke and she'll bring it along in a few minutes. Laura settles for the coffee and fills her cup from the plastic thermos.

After the first sip, she attempts to relax. She flexes and unflexes her fingers and arches the tension out of her back with several lifts and drops of her shoulders. She looks around and notices that the plastic covering on the overstuffed back-rest of her booth is coming apart at the seams and its mottled-grey intestines are oozing out.

Ridiculously, she immediately feels kinship with the booth. She thinks that too much had been expected of it, so it finally gave up trying to hold everything together. And, because it failed to keep things as they were, it was shoved off in disgrace to a seldom used corner of the diner. She thinks of the many ways in which she herself has always tried to hold everything together: *Hannah, dear, don't forget your dental appointment. Kevin — your briefcase.* She had rolled matching socks into each other, removed pill balls from sweaters with adhesive tape measured off into two-inch lengths, and sipped the morning milk to see if it was sour before it ended up on Hannah's cereal or curdled in Kevin's coffee.

When she sets her cup down on the arborite table she notices that the plastic outer coating of the table top has been gouged, as if some curious customer wanted to dig out the peppering of multi-coloured confetti that had been layered just underneath. She thinks that this sprinkling of confetti was probably a decorator's ploy to camouflage stains and splotches, and that it most likely worked before the surface became so pock-marked. She wonders whether the curious customer who had picked and jabbed at the plastic had wanted to find out for himself whether the confetti was made of paper or paint chips. This thought triggers a memory of Lucy O'Grady.

Laura smiles, remembering Lucy, her friend in fourth grade. Lucy, a Catholic girl straight from Ireland, had sat beside her in school. She always wore what looked like a miniature pin cushion fastened to her cotton undershirt. It was a little white satin sack with a red crocheted edging. Laura had wondered what mysteries this sack contained. Even in gym class, Lucy was careful to pin it to the inside of her blouse. One day, curiosity got the better of Laura and she asked Lucy about it. Lucy had explained that it contained a holy relic. When pressed for details, Lucy confided, in a hushed voice as if she were in church or at a wake, that the piece of wax inside was a fragment of a candle that was stamped with the image of the Lamb of God, and that it had been blessed by the Pope.

"Let's tear it open," Laura had wheedled when they got back to the classroom. She was now infinitely more curious because of the fear and awe in Lucy's voice. She had urged impatiently, "We can always sew it back together. It will only take a few stitches."

Probably more because of Lucy's need for a friend than her need to satisfy her own curiosity, Lucy had begun ripping and tearing away at the tiny silk threads of the sack. For scissors she had used the point of the gold safety pin that fastened the relic to her shirt. In seconds she had ransacked the little pouch completely and dumped the contents — a tiny splinter of candle — onto her social studies text book.

Lucy had stared at the candle chip as if she were mesmerized, and then a terrified look had settled over her face, as if she had just desecrated a burial ground and was now waiting for the spirits of the dead to seek their revenge. Wordlessly, she had reclaimed the scrap of wax from the text book and wrapped it up in the tattered satin covering and then wildly looked around her, explaining there was no place sacred enough to dispose of the stuff so she would have to carry the bits and pieces in her hand all day. She had explained, her voice hopeless, that only fire would be an acceptable form of destruction. But there was no place to get fire in the school, or for that matter at her home, because they lived in an apartment over a store in the downtown section of Fredericton, and the apartment had oil heating.

Laura is still thinking about Lucy when Hannah slides into the seat opposite her.

"Grungy," she says. "Real grungy." Laura doesn't ask whether she is referring to the bathroom specifically or to the diner as a whole. All she says in reply is, "It's been around for as long as I can remember."

The waitress brings over Hannah's fries and pop, and a fresh thermos of coffee for Laura. Laura refills her cup from the thermos and Hannah picks at her food.

As Laura watches Hannah cull through her fries, she asks the question that has never left her mind since Hannah threw the words on the car seat earlier in the morning. And she asks it so suddenly that she astounds herself as well as Hannah. "How did you find out about Claude and me?"

Hannah, caught off guard, sucks in a small startled breath, as if she has come upon something distasteful in the fries.

Laura had every intention of leaving Hannah's words on the seat, exactly where they had been thrown. Over the years, she has conditioned herself to skirt the unpleasant, to turn a blind eye. Now, she can't believe that she has asked the question for which she is not sure she wants an answer.

"I need to know," she ventures. "We can't just pretend you never said what you said."

Hannah, recovering quickly, rolls her eyes upward, making a face as if she will retch all over the table if this conversation doesn't come to an immediate halt.

"Not here!" she snarls, darting a furtive look behind her to see if anyone is within hearing range. "Not here!"

Laura ignores the dramatics and says insistently, "You were the one who brought this up. I have a right to know how you found out."

Although she speaks calmly, her heart is galloping so hard she thinks that, any second, her arteries may break and blood will saturate her tee-shirt. Since the very instant she rallied from the shock of hearing Hannah's words about Claude, Laura has wondered how Hannah found out about the affair. Her mind has raced through the different ways this could have happened and has found all of the ways unacceptable. And, although every fiber in her body recoils at the very thought of learning how Hannah has uncovered her secret, she is like a person who searches a dark basement for a prowler — not wanting to find one, but unable to rest until one is found. She repeats her demand, and this time is more emphatic. "I *do* have the right to know."

"Right!" Hannah scoffs. Again she rolls her eyes upward as if she has never heard anything so outrageous. "You have the *right*? Give me a break."

Once more Laura ignores Hannah's dramatics. She speaks severely, not only to let Hannah know that she intends to get an answer, but to keep her voice from trembling.

"Hannah, I intend to know how you found out about us. So tell me now!"

The use of the pronoun "us," which falls so easily off Laura's lips and links her mother with the man who is cuckholding her father, enrages Hannah. She speaks through clenched teeth. "Not that *dirt* here!" She spits out the word as if it is some disgusting offal she can't wait to get off her lips.

Laura's back instantly arches, as if a dagger has been plunged in her back. "*Dirt!*" she says, and pushes forward in the booth so that she is only inches from Hannah's face. "*Dirt!*" she repeats, and hears the word scuttling off her lips like a blasphemy. How dare this child of hers call her precious moments with Claude "dirt!" Her hand, which had been reaching for her coffee cup, jerks back as if instinctively readying itself to slap Hannah across the mouth to stuff the filthy word back in her throat, back where it belongs. She raises her hand and tries to bring it forward to make contact with Hannah's face, but she can't budge it from its position in mid-air. It is as if an unseen force is gripping it, holding it in check, preventing it from striking Hannah in scourging outrage. After a second or two, her hand drops back down on the table, an impotent mound of flesh. She stares incredulously at it. The shame and horror of her thwarted intention makes her body break out in a cold sweat. Her head begins to pound. The pain is so severe that it feels as if her brain is rubbing raw and unprotected against her skull. She begins to tremble so violently that, to steady herself, she places one arm over the other, imprisoning both limbs on the table.

After a few moments she musters the strength to get up and leave the diner. She hurriedly reaches for her sweater and purse and then rummages in her wallet and pulls out a ten dollar bill and tosses it on the table. "I'll be in the car," she says shakily, pausing just long enough at the edge of the booth to pull herself together so that when she walks across the floor the two men sitting at the far end of the diner will have no idea of the rage that is swirling around inside her. Nor will they have any idea of the shame that is forcing the rage out of the way.

After she is seated in the car her body continues to tremble. Sweat pours off her face, even though she still feels chilled to the bone. She pulls on her sweater and then reaches up with the palm of her hand and swipes at her face, wiping away the sweat that is oozing up through her Cover Girl make-up — a gift from her mother who, since retiring to Vancouver, has moved away from Ponds Vanishing Cream and Lily of the Valley body powder.

As she waits for Hannah, she wonders what force had held her hand in check. What force had prevented her from violently striking out at her daughter? She wonders whether it was simply her well-developed sense of decorum, brought about by a mother who had drilled her on proper etiquette in public, or whether, in fact, it was some primal protective force that had prevented her from carrying out an action she would forever regret. She decides it was the latter — the primal force. She remembers an earlier time, when she had reacted in a similar instinctive manner to protect Hannah. That time, though, instead of immobilizing her body, the instinct had readied it for action.

She recalls that time clearly. It was when Hannah was three years old. They were in New Mexico, where Kevin was doing summer sessional teaching. Laura was out in their yard hanging out clothes, and Hannah was following Laura around as she pulled the wet clothes from the basket and hung them on the umbrella-type clothes line. She had dropped a clothespin, and when she stooped down to pick it up she saw a snake within inches of Hannah's bare heel, poised, as she believed, to strike. Although Laura, too, was in her bare feet, she didn't waver for an instant. She jumped on the head of that snake and stomped it to death. As it turned out, the snake was only a harmless creature, but Laura knew she would have killed it without a moment's hesitation even if it had been a boa constrictor.

Hannah slouches back to the car, a scowl on her face, her tote bag straddling her shoulders as if it is a knapsack. Her crested University of Laval sweater is tied by the arms around her waist. She slides in over the seat and settles herself in much the same way as she had when they started off from Fredericton, her back half turned to her mother.

"Face me, Hannah," Laura says abruptly, her leashed-in anger putting steel in her spine. "We're going to talk whether you like it or not."

"I don't like it," Hannah retorts, making no move to comply. "And I don't have to talk about what I don't want to talk about. I think that's still permitted in Canada."

Laura speaks in a level voice, her words low in her throat. She knows she holds the trump card. "If you want me to drive you the rest of the way, you have to talk to me." She cavalierly flails one hand in the direction of Fredericton and the other towards Quebec. "North, south, east, west makes no never mind difference to me. It's up to you."

Hannah spins around to confront Laura, a disbelieving look on her face. "Don't be ridiculous, Mother," she says, her voice riddled with disgust. "Let's stop wasting time. I'd like to get to the dorm before dark."

Laura grabs the car keys from her purse and plunges them so deep into the ignition that it grinds in protest. "Either we're going to talk or I'm going to turn around and drop you off at Hartland. A bus should be along sometime before the day is over."

Hannah's eyes register confusion, bewilderment. She waits for a moment — waits for some tip that Laura, as usual, is bluffing and will back down. But Laura just stares back at her, unwavering.

To her immense confoundment, Hannah realizes that there is no bluff and that she will have to capitulate. She determines not to do so gracefully.

"Then let's get out of here," she snarls. "Whatever it is you want to know about how I discovered your scummy little affair with your precious Clot, I'll tell you." She makes another face as if she is going to lose her lunch. "It's enough to make a person barf."

"His name is Claude, Hannah," Laura says coolly, not allow-ing her anger to unsettle her. "We've spent enough on French tutors for you to pronounce that correctly." She pauses purpose-fully at the entrance to the highway, as if she can just as easily retrace their journey as keep on with it. "Now let's start over again. Please tell me how you found out about us."

"If you mean was I out spying on *us*, I wasn't," Hannah retorts sarcastically, trying to save face and buckle under at the same time. She twists around once more to face Laura, her eyes blazing with anger and defiance.

"I asked you, how did you find out about us?" Laura repeats levelly, looking down the highway instead of up, as though she is about to head homeward.

Hannah immediately abandons her fencing. "I found that sick, gross letter he wrote you. That's how I found out." She simulates Claude's voice, or what she would have Laura believe is Claude's voice, a fawning sickly-sweet tone — an effeminate tone. She gestures nicely with her hands. "My Precious Laura."

Laura winces visibly. Cold rushes over her flesh. She feels as if her skin is shrinking under the weight of Hannah's insinuating voice. She wishes she could put her hands over her ears and shut out the insults, like she used to do when she was a child and people talked about things that repulsed her, such as shooting deer in the fall or trapping beaver. But now she refuses to give in to her squeamishness and prods impatiently, hustling Hannah along as if hurrying the disclosure will make it easier to bear. "Where? Tell me where."

Hannah deliberately misinterprets. "Where what?" she snaps. "Macquapit Lake I s'pose. His place. Our place. My bedroom. Dad's bedroom. How am I supposed to know where you carried on! It was your slimy little affair."

Again Laura winces, and again she refuses to be put off. "I mean where was the letter?"

Although the wince isn't lost on Hannah, she is also aware that Laura is still poised at the highway entrance, ready to point the car in either the direction of Quebec City or Fredericton.

Knowing she has been bested, she sullenly reveals the information, her voice throwing her words out as if they are bullets. "When I came out to the cottage after I got back from Vancouver and you had mislaid your house keys. And we had to go searching for them. I found it then ..." She gives Laura the full benefit of a pregnant pause. "... In your lingerie drawer."

Without further hesitation, Laura pulls out onto the highway and heads toward Quebec. She clearly remembers the day Hannah is speaking about. And she had indeed hidden Claude's letter in her lingerie drawer. Like Lucy O'Grady with her mutilated relic, she had felt there was no place sacred enough to put the letter. She couldn't bear to tear it up, yet she hadn't dared to carry it in her purse in case she were ever in an accident, so she had placed it in her lingerie drawer, well hidden underneath mounds of panties and bras. She had felt safe with it there. It was easy to get at in case of fire, and yet it was not a place where either Kevin or Hannah was likely to browse.

"And you read it?" she reproaches, already knowing the answer because Hannah has quoted correctly from the letter's salutation. Her tone intimates that Hannah should have known better than to rob someone of their privacy.

"Of course I read it," Hannah retorts, defensively.

They snarl words at each other, each one staring straight ahead at the road, not daring to meet the other's eyes.

Hannah's mouth puckers, as if she has eaten something tainted with rot. "How did I know it would be something so gross," she says, still looking straight ahead. "I just thought it was probably something else you had mislaid, the way you had it pushed underneath your stuff. I almost gagged when I read it."

Laura pictures Hannah reading the letter. She sees her shock, her disillusionment, her fear. And she realizes that it is as much fear as disgust that is now making her daughter's words so caustic. Laura's emotions tumble around in confusion. Anger and love. Love and anger.

Suddenly, instead of continuing to chastise Hannah for breeching her privacy, Laura now aches to hug her, to reassure her, just as she used to do when Hannah was small and had awakened from a frightening nightmare. Her arms almost tremble from their need to make gentle contact with Hannah's flesh. But she knows that Hannah will shuck off her embrace now, just as she used to shuck it off back then.

She remembers how, as a child, Hannah would always squirm out of her arms and run to Kevin, although Laura had been the first one to hear the child's needy cry. Laura had always been the one to get up out of bed and go into Hannah's room, while Kevin slept through the child's cries. The slightest noise from the nursery had always aroused Laura, as if she were only cat-napping, waiting for sounds from Hannah. But usually the commotion of Laura getting out of bed would be enough to rouse Kevin from his sleep, and he would then come padding barefoot across the hall. Hannah's arms would always sidestep Laura's and immediately reach for Kevin's, knowing he would bring her into their bedroom — an act Laura disapproved of. Kevin would sing Hannah a lullabye — always the same old-fashioned one. She wonders if Hannah still remembers: *Tell me the tales that to you were so true. Long, long ago. Long ago.*

"I'm really sorry, Hannah," Laura says now, settling for words instead of touches, and surprising Hannah with her abrupt turn-about. "I'm sorry you had to find out that way. I'm sorry you had to find out at all."

Hannah is not so easily won over. Totally discounting the contrition, she hauls her shoulders into a self-righteous huff and says threateningly, "I should have told Dad. I should have showed the letter to him. I just didn't want to hurt him. But I think it's about time he knew what's been going on."

Laura stiffens and her next words totally collapse Hannah's attempt at a threat. "Go ahead and tell him. It wouldn't upset him as much as you think. Trust me, it wouldn't."

Hannah swallows hard, bewildered by Laura's disclosure. "What?!" she says, not sure she has heard correctly. She darts a hurried look at Laura, certain she'll see by her face that she's rattled and is trying to bluff. But Laura shows no signs of agitation.

Aghast, Hannah almost shouts, "You mean you've told him already? You've actually confessed?"

Suddenly, the announcement over the Thanksgiving table about the marriage breakup becomes instantly understandable. "That's it, isn't it?" Hannah crows exultantly, as if a great mystery has been unveiled. "You already told him. That's why the divorce."

Laura shakes her head and says honestly, aware she is making herself vulnerable, "He doesn't know about the letter. Or about Claude. But I'm certain it wouldn't matter to him even if he did." She pauses a moment and then retracts, "But he'd care about it going public. He's in line for the Dean's job. He doesn't want that jeopardized."

Laura considers making a clean breast of how things are between her and Kevin. She wavers only an instant and then says, "The fact is, Hannah, our marriage — your father's and mine — came to an end long before that letter." She stretches out the word, "L-o-n-g before that letter."

Hannah tosses her head scornfully and the look on her face says that she doesn't believe a word of what Laura has just said. She is still convinced her mother's calmness is a bluff — a bluff which she intends to call. Sporting a cunning smile, she taunts, her voice intentionally silky, "If you're so sure it won't bother him in the least that his wife's running around, I'll save you the trouble and tell him for you. I'll phone him as soon as I get to the dormitory." She gives a foxy over-the-shoulder glance at Laura.

Laura disappoints her by still showing no signs of alarm. "I spoke the truth when I said it wouldn't bother him." She says this calmly, surprising herself at how easily she can say it, and with what little pain. "Our marriage is over. But, like I said, your father doesn't want our dirty linen aired in public. And I respect that. That's one reason I didn't flaunt my relationship with Claude. But the main reason I was hiding that letter was to keep you from being hurt." Tentatively, she reaches her hand out towards Hannah, but pulls it back before it touches her.

Hannah rights herself in the seat, and gives Laura the full brunt of her scorn. "Sure! Sure!" she scoffs. "There's about as much truth in that as you saying you're not getting a divorce to go after ... after ... after *him*." She stutters over Claude's name, not daring to butcher it again, yet not willing to dignify him with one that isn't butchered. "I can't believe you're going to divorce Dad for *him!*"

Laura's patience gives way. "Then don't," she snaps. "But I'm telling you for the last time *he* has nothing to do with the trouble between your father and me." She pauses a second before adding, "And don't blame the education grant either. The break-up would have happened anyway." She cements this statement with another one. "And it should have happened years earlier." She lifts one finger from the wheel, and then another — as if to count how many years earlier it should have happened — and then abruptly tosses this idea aside as being too tedious. "Trust me," she says bluntly, leaving no doubt for mistrust, "the marriage was worn out for more years than I care to add up. And that's the God's truth."

Hannah squirms in her seat, not happy with the direction the conversation is taking. The last thing she wants to hear is the truth, especially if the truth isn't to her liking. She halts the conversation by looking out through the car window and pointing to a grey van ahead of them.

"Look at him — that's your furniture truck, or whatever," she says, desperately trying to veer off the subject of her parents' unsuitable marriage. "The one with 'Bell' on the side. Haven't we passed him twice already?"

Laura looks out and acknowledges that indeed they did pass the same truck earlier. Then she quickly returns to the subject at hand, well aware that what she is going to say is not something Hannah is prepared to hear. But then, she knows there are volumes of information Hannah is not prepared to hear — for example, that Claude had made Laura realize she is still a vital, alive and lustful woman, and that the splendour of those days at Macquapit Lake is something she will savour forever. And Hannah is not prepared to hear that, for the first time in her life, her mother knows what it is to truly love someone and to have that someone love her in return. Mostly, though, Hannah is not prepared to hear that, for Laura, the summer of '91 had been far too long in coming.

But Laura cannot fault Hannah for not wanting to hear such things. Indeed, even if she did want to hear them, Laura thinks, there is no way a mother can share such intimate moments with a daughter, especially a daughter who favours her father. But there are things she can tell Hannah — *ought* to tell her — and, if not in detail, at least in an abridged form. She thinks it is now time that Hannah knew the truth about her parents' marriage — or at least an edited version of the truth. She will leave the unedited version for Kevin to parcel out, should he ever wish to do so.

"Your father and I should have separated years ago." Laura says this coolly, knowing that Hannah probably won't believe what she is saying now, any more than she believes what Laura had said about Kevin's lack of caring about her affair. She forbids herself to get upset if Hannah doesn't believe her. "And, like I already said, we should never have gotten married in the first place. We've both known that for a very long time."

Hannah reacts as Laura expected.

"I don't believe you," she snaps, "not for a minute." However, it is obvious to Laura that Hannah does believe, because she rolls down the window on her side of the car as if there's not enough air, as if she suddenly can't breathe. Then, as if the fresh air has revived her, she turns her full face to Laura, and with a mocking smile on her lips she chides, "And I suppose the next thing you'll try and tell me is that Dad had an affair."

Although Hannah has set herself up for a reply, she doesn't want to hear one. She quickly intercepts anything Laura is about to say by letting her know that it would be a waste of breath, unless what she says is in Kevin's favour. "Don't bother telling me," Hannah says, waving her hands dismissively. "I wouldn't believe you even if you showed me pictures. I'd know you were just trying to find someone else to blame. You want to leave, but you don't want to shoulder the blame."

Laura clenches her hands so tightly on the steering wheel that her fingers hurt. It is as if she tries to block out one pain with another. It surprises her that Hannah's cruel words can hurt so much, even when she is prepared for them, even when she is convinced she is inured to them. Certainly, there is no reason why Hannah's attitude should shock her. Laura has always known that in any confrontation between her and Kevin, Hannah's allegiance would be with Kevin. It has never been otherwise, and probably never will be otherwise. She wonders now, as she has often wondered before, why she has failed to cement her bond with this child.

Whenever she has ruminated on this lack of cementing, Laura has always arrived at the conclusion that in order to claim Hannah's loyalty away from Kevin she would have had to be either stronger or weaker — strong enough to be feared or weak enough to be pitied. And she had been neither. And, too, she has often wondered if, early on, she had thrown herself on her daughter's mercy and wailed over her arid, passionless marriage, would this flaunting of deprivation have gained Hannah's pity? But because she has never wanted Hannah's love to come to her out of either fear or pity, she has kept her marital problems under close cover. Besides, in fairness to herself, she has never had any desire to hog Hannah's loyalty all to herself. All she has ever wanted was to be allowed to share it with Kevin.

Sometimes, when she is being brutally honest with herself, Laura allows that the fault for Hannah's resentment of her lies solely within herself. She has always been too stingy in showing her affections for this child. Indeed, she thinks she has been miserly to the point of parsimony. And she has been covetous.

She recalls, for example, one evening when Kevin had been sitting in the den reading the paper. She had been sitting opposite him, in the rocking chair, knitting a sweater for one of Hannah's dolls — an angora sweater in hot pink that Hannah claimed was an essential addition to any doll's wardrobe. Hannah was about five. She was sitting on the floor lacerating the pages of *Chatelaine* magazine with her snub-nosed scissors. She needed pictures of four healthy foods for her kindergarten project — a project that would be pasted up on the school bulletin board the next day. In the midst of cutting out a picture of a bunch of carrots, Hannah suddenly tired of the job and dropped the scissors and ran to Kevin and climbed upon his knee. He acknowledged her by giving her a hard, playful hug before going back to his reading. Hannah just sat there, solidly contented, totally complacent, her arm around Kevin's neck as if his love was hers for the taking whenever the mood hit her.

Starving for a hug, Laura had looked on covetously at the two of them, so secure, so complete. For a full minute or more she had watched, desperately envying the ease with which Hannah was always able to claim Kevin's affections. Then, suddenly, as if her own need for a caress had become overwhelming, she dropped her knitting on the floor and, with a mountain of trepidation, went and sat on Kevin's other knee.

"Hey, you two," Kevin had said, surprised enough to drop the newspaper. Then, in a voice that was only slightly joking, he had fussed, "I'm not the strong man of the circus. I can't hold both of you at the same time."

Hannah, not willing to be displaced by Laura, petulantly pushed at her mother's shoulder. "I was here first, Mommie. You get off."

As if in response to Hannah's request, Kevin's knee, the one Laura was sitting on, went slack. She got off and went back to her chair, and as she was about to sit down she had locked eyes with Hannah. The child had smiled at her — a triumphant smile, Laura thought. That night, when she was tucking Hannah into bed, she could only give the child a cursory kiss, a cursory hug. Afterwards, she had felt so guilty she couldn't sleep, and finally, in the middle of the night, she had climbed out of bed and gone to Hannah's room. She had bent over the child and kissed her, and Hannah, sleeping soundly, had shaken her head as if a fly had crawled on her forehead.

And there were other such times when she had been covetous of Hannah's abiltiy to exact love from Kevin — more times, she thinks, than she can recall. And more times, she hopes, than Hannah can recall.

As if reading her thoughts, Hannah turns around in her seat, faces Laura and says, cruelly honest, "All the time I was growing up I loved Dad best."

Although this revelation of Hannah's is also not news, it still cuts Laura to the quick, but because she doesn't want Hannah to know how deeply she has been stabbed, she manages a matter-of-fact response, "I've always known that. So what else is new?"

She says this with much forced easiness, as if the subject is as remote as the rainforest in Brazil and equally unconnected to her. She continues, "And for what it's worth, I always believed he loved you best, too. Yes, I'm certain he did. Still does, for that matter."

But once she hears her words spoken out loud — acknowledging that she has never received a fair share of Kevin's love — she realizes that the speech from her own mouth has hurt her far worse than the words Hannah has spoken. Tears well up in her eyes and she blinks hard to make them disappear. On only one other occasion has she ever acknowledged to another person — and that was to Claude — that she has always been severely lonely inside her marriage, always severely deprived of love. Aware now that she is again making herself vulnerable, but suddenly not caring about keeping up a stalwart front, she confesses, "I often felt alien when the three of us were together. I felt like an outsider. I always felt unneeded. Except, of course, to keep the domestic things going."

She then adds, with a small laugh that is too brittle to carry her humour, "But at least I didn't have to ask that question about the canoe tipping over and who would he save, you or me. I just told myself I had better learn to swim or I'd be food for the fish."

Her words end on an unexpected catch, and because she doesn't want Hannah to accuse her of mining for pity, she curtly refers back to Hannah's accusation that she is trying to lay the blame for the marriage break-up solely on Kevin. "I've no intention of blaming your father totally for the mess of our marriage. So I'll thank you not to accuse me of that! And I'd be the last person to deny that he's been an excellent father to you. An excellent provider. And to me, for that matter. As far as material things go." She takes a deep breath and finishes, "But I also want you to understand I'm not the villain you're trying to make me out to be, either. It was just a marriage that should never have been."

Once more there is silence in the car. In this space Laura remembers the person she was before her marriage. She is sure that her union with Kevin has sucked the blitheness from her life. And she is sure that it has made her what she is, or what she had become before Claude — a woman as dry and as juiceless as a wad of cotton, a woman so parched for love that she was willing to steal it from her own daughter.

Just as, earlier on, Laura wished that she could open up her life fully to Hannah and tell her what meeting Claude has meant to her, she now wishes she could describe to Hannah what the girlish Laura was like, and tell her of the picture she always held in her mind of the ideal mother she intended to become. She wishes she could make pictures in words and sentences — pictures of the impetuous, flighty young girl who stayed out on her high school graduation night because she had never seen the sun come up, or of the impish teenager who had helped to paint the flagpole of a rival school with her own school colours. She wishes she could tell Hannah that she knows she has fallen far short of the mother she always imagined she would be. And, more importantly, she wishes she could explain why she thinks she has fallen so short. But there is so much she can't tell Hannah without explaining to her the sequence of events that led to that afternoon when she knew with certainty that she had lain for years in a queen-sized bed beside a man who didn't love her — a man who was not capable of loving her in the way she needed to be loved, in the way she deserved to be loved; a man who, over the years, had become a polite, civilized stranger to her. As, for that matter, she had become to him.

In this same silence, and as if in reflection, Hannah realizes the enormity of what she said earlier about loving her father best, and wants to dilute its pain for Laura. She asks civilly, for the moment keeping her anger in check, "Then, tell me, why did you and Dad get married if you shouldn't have?"

Laura replies without hesitation, surprising herself with her unhedged answer, "Because I was pregnant." She says this bluntly, suddenly tired of years and years of stringing sentences together with benign lies, and weary of measuring out information in varnished truth.

Hannah snaps a look at Laura, her eyes flashing with both shock and anger.

"You were pregnant *before* you got married?" Her words are stained with incredulity. She then quickly sums up the meaning of this new information in terms of herself. She thumbs her chest and says accusingly, "So you're saying it's my fault you got married because you were pregnant with me. At least now I know why you always resented me."

Laura says nothing for a few seconds. She concentrates on passing the van in front of her. After she is safely back in her own lane, she speaks, her voice dropping as if a child is sleeping nearby, "I wasn't pregnant with you, Hannah. Another baby. But I miscarried early on in the pregnancy."

Hannah is so stunned that she opens her mouth to form words but no sound comes out. She tries a second time and stammers, "I never ... nobody told me ... you never said." Then, either because she is moved by the softness in her mother's voice, or because she is relieved that the blame for the union of Laura and Kevin cannot be placed on her, or perhaps because of a force so primal it might have sprung from her womb, she reaches out her hand and tentatively touches Laura's arm, forming a woman to woman connection. "Oh, Mom. I'm sorry. I really am."

Hannah's compassion is so unexpected that Laura's eyes sting again with tears, and once more she has to blink hard to beat them back. She blinks back the tears, not only because she has to see the road, but in case the sight of her mother weeping may be so off-putting to Hannah that she will put a halt to the conversation that is just beginning to take wing.

"I was ashamed to tell you," Laura confesses quietly, knowing she is once more leaving herself vulnerable. "And I was afraid. I thought you'd turn away from me altogether. I thought you'd never listen to my advice if you knew what a mess I'd made of my own life."

As if floodgates have been opened, as if she has finally released the plastic raincoat from its confining pouch and never intends to stuff it back in again, words and sentences tumble headlong out of her mouth.

"We never talked about it, your father and I. Not after it happened. And your grandparents didn't either. It wasn't a conspiracy or anything. It wasn't as if we all said, we mustn't tell Hannah. It just evolved that way. But the truth is we wouldn't have gotten married if I hadn't been pregnant. Or if I had any inkling I was going to miscarry." She adds, her voice even softer than before, "It was a boy. At least we're pretty sure it was. Mary/Joseph. That was his name. I started to miscarry right after my wedding. On the way to Halifax. Your father was frightened to death. He was so inexperienced with anything like that. We both were. It's not something either of us is likely to forget."

F i v e

A half hour after Reverend Bradscome pronounced Laura and Kevin Stevenson husband and wife, they were on their way to Halifax. Their car had been packed the night before and they had booked a hotel in Moncton because they intended to spend their wedding night there and then drive on to Nova Scotia the next day. But even during the marriage ceremony, Laura had felt so tired she wished they had made plans to stay in Fredericton until morning. The nap her mother had insisted she take early in the afternoon hadn't helped any, and she had awakened feeling more drained than when she had gone to bed. In fact, she had felt so weak that when Kevin placed the wedding ring — a narrow white-gold band — on her finger, it was as if he had weighted her down with a rock. She had leaned against Janet, her maid of honour, to keep from falling headlong into Reverend Bradscome.

They were no sooner on the road to Moncton than her labor started. It was just a twinge or two at first, just enough to make her think she shouldn't have taken a second helping of her mother's crab salad. But then the pains progressed, and soon she was haemorrhaging. By the time they reached the outskirts of the city, she was loosing blood so rapidly that, terrified, Kevin pulled to the side of the road and rummaged through the pile of household stuff in the trunk of the car for blankets. He helped her get into the back seat and wrapped her up, making sure her legs were elevated. But still the blood kept flowing. Just inside the city limits he found a service station and asked directions to the nearest hospital.

Laura had lost consciousness by then, and when she woke up hours later she was in Hotel Dieu Hospital and Kevin was wiping her sweat-soaked hair with a handful of tissues he had pulled from a box on her nightstand.

"The baby?" she whispered frantically as soon as she opened her eyes, rubbing her stomach as if she would be able to discern the presence or absence of the child through the cotton hospital gown.

Kevin dropped the damp tissues on the bed and busied himself with the sleeves of his sweater, turning the cuffs up and then down.

"It's gone," he said, not meeting her eyes and still fumbling with his sweater sleeves. "There was nothing they could do."

She turned her face to the wall and shut her eyes tight.

"It's my fault," she whispered. "It's what I had wished for in the clinic. It's what I had hoped would happen when they told me."

Kevin scolded, but not very harshly. "You're being ridiculous." He gently rubbed his fingers over her impaled hand, careful to skirt the intravenous needle. But ever the scientist, ever interested in presenting facts, he then explained that a miscarriage is usually nature's way of ridding the womb of an imperfect fetus. "It had nothing to do with your wishing for a miscarriage. It's nature's way. It expels what shouldn't survive."

He fumbled some more with his sweater sleeves and then stood up, rammed his hands into his pockets and paced around the bed several times as if his life was spinning out of control and he was trying to find a way to keep it on track. When he sat back down on the bed again he said, without looking at her, as if he were talking to himself, "But if it had to happen, why couldn't it have happened earlier? We wouldn't have had to get married ..." After what seemed an interminable silence, he added, "in such a rush."

She didn't know then, and never asked later, whether the break in his sentence was caused by the appearance of a nurse bearing a hypodermic needle or whether the phrase had been tacked on to temper the bitter taste of truth. In any event, his words opened up a wound in her heart, a wound that would be kept raw with the help of other circumstances.

The nurse's injection kept Laura asleep for several hours, and when she woke up the first thing she saw was a vase of red roses sitting on the tray at the foot of her bed. Against the white of the bedspread, their bitter redness resembled a pool of freshly-spilled blood. She eased herself up in the bed and reached over her empty stomach for the card that was tucked between the long lean stems. Kevin's card. After she read it, she laid it back down and pulled one of the partly unfurled rose buds out of the vase. She brought it to her lips.

"I'm sorry," she crooned softly, looking at the delicate leaves curled into each other so tight and snug. "They shouldn't have plucked you before your time. You never got to feel the sunshine on your face. And you weren't even imperfect."

She then carefully placed the bud back with the other roses and gingerly inched herself back down in bed. The minute she lay down, an unbidden thought flashed through her mind: How does a hospital get rid of an imperfect fetus? She pictured a cemetery in a country churchyard. Daisies were blooming and a gentle breeze was rippling through the clover. She saw a tiny marble lamb resting beside a mound of freshly-turned earth. She squeezed her eyes shut to hold the image, feeling the soft grass underneath her bare feet and tasting the sweetness of the white clover — even smelling the moist warmth of the newly broken sod.

But despite her efforts, the image disappeared and in its place she saw an incinerator — Dante's inferno. Baby parts were blistering in the heat and giving off a stench so strong her stomach contracted. When she tried to halt these pictures, other ones, more terrible ones, moved in to take their place. She saw plastic bags — green plastic garbage bags. They were piled up in the city dump, filled to the neck with operating room refuse, mostly baby parts — arms, fingers, toes, legs. Grey gulls soared overhead, their beady eyes searching for rips and tears in the plastic.

She then heard piercing screams, and only when two nurses came rushing into her room did she realize that the screams were coming from her own throat. She kept on screaming, unable to stop and unable to separate her dream from reality.

"The gulls," she cried. "They're eating my baby." Other whitecoated people quickly filled the room, and even as she felt the prick of still another needle being jabbed into her already needle-pricked arm, she hollered, "My baby's in a garbage bag — in the city dump."

The next time she woke up, a nursing sister — a nun who was dressed in a white habit and who, she later learned, was a member of the Sisters of Mercy Order — was sitting beside her bed.

"You had a nice little snooze," the nun said, her voice soothing. Laura's eyes instantly darted wildly around the room trying to get her bearings. Sister Cornelia introduced herself. "I'm Sister Cornelia and I've been sitting with you for a while now, watching you sleep. You're in our hospital."

Sister Cornelia then got up from her chair and went to Laura's bedside table and picked up a glass of water and a straw and brought them over to her. "Just a sip," she advised, helping her to prop herself up in bed. "Any more and your stomach will turn."

Obediently, Laura sipped the tepid water as her eyes searched the room for Kevin.

As if reading her thoughts, Sister Cornelia explained. "Your husband just left. I sent him off to the cafeteria. He hasn't left your side all day."

Gradually, Laura felt the room coming into focus, and with it the unruly scene she had made earlier came flooding back. Embarrassed, she tried to apologize.

"I kicked up a stupid fuss," she mumbled. "I don't know what got into me."

Sister Cornelia stood up and righted Laura's pillows, pummelling them into softness before stacking them behind her neck. "I should think anyone who had just been told their child died would be entitled to make a stupid fuss if they wanted to," she said in a matter-of-fact voice, relieving Laura's discomposure. "Especially if they were full of sedatives."

She then reached deep into the pocket of her habit and pulled out a small indigo blue velvet case, the type of case that can be found in jewelry stores for holding pearls or necklaces.

"They told me you were worried about what happened to your baby's remains," she said, snapping open the case to expose an ivory satin interior. She smoothed a pale finger over the satin and explained to Laura that she had been in the operating theater when they brought her in.

"Just look at this," she urged. "It's so snug in here." She tipped the case so Laura could see. "Just right for a Holy Innocent."

Laura said nothing, just looked at the empty jewelry box, confusion registering in her eyes. Sister Cornelia explained. "We save the little unborn souls. And we baptize them and give them a Christian burial."

She snapped the case shut and dropped it back into her pocket. "Oh, some of the doctors laugh at us," she explained, smiling a serene smile at the ignorance of the doctors. "They think it's a lot of malarkey. They say they're aborted fetuses, not souls. Some even call them embryos. But we pay no attention. We baptize them anyway. And that's why we always carry with us into the theater a little bottle of holy water as well as the cases." She plunged her hand once more into her pocket and produced a small bottle of water. "Holy water," she explained as she unscrewed the cap and tipped the bottle so that a few drops of water fell on the back of her hand. "We let a few drops fall on the child and say, 'I baptise you Mary/Joseph in the name of the Father and of the Son and of the Holy Spirit.' Simple as that. We call all of the children Mary/Joseph unless we clearly know whether its a boy or a girl. Or if we're in too much of a hurry to go looking. But if we know, we just say Mary or Joseph, whichever is suitable." She added, as she safely settled the bottle of holy water back down into the deep habit pocket, "Your baby was called Mary/Joseph."

She went on to explain that some of the jewelry stores and many parishioners saved pretty boxes to give to the hospital for this purpose.

She stood up to leave. As she smoothed out the bedspread where she had leaned up against it, she said soothingly, "Now, Laura, dear. Don't go fretting about your little one. We took the little soul to Mr. Robichaud's mortuary. He always finds someone to take our unborns to Heaven. He just slips the box into someone else's casket. He told me he had someone being buried tomorrow. Early in the morning. With a Mass of Requiem, no less. A good send-off, eh! A Mr. LeBlanc."

Because complications arose, Laura had to stay in the hospital longer than expected, and rather than have Kevin be late for his classes, she insisted that he go on to Nova Scotia without her.

"Mother'll drive me to Halifax when I get out," she assured him. "There's no need for you to hang around."

Five days later, while she was waiting for her mother to pick her up, she released herself from the hospital and went in search of Mr. LeBlanc's grave. First she took a taxi to the library, got the back issues of the *Moncton Tribune* and searched the obituaries. Within a few minutes, she came upon the item she wanted.

> *LeBlanc, Denis L. Peacefully at his home in Moncton on Tuesday after a courageous battle with cancer. Beloved husband of Marie (Chiasson). In addition to his widow, Mr. LeBlanc leaves to mourn two sons, Marc and Denis, both of Moncton.*
>
> *The body is resting at Robichaud's Funeral Home, 100 Germaine Street. The funeral will be held on Friday morning at nine-thirty, at Sts. Peter and Paul Church, with a Funeral Mass. Interment will take place in St. Joseph's Cemetery. Visiting on Wednesday and Thursday, from two to four p.m., and seven to nine p.m.*

Laura took another taxi to St. Joseph's Cemetery and asked the caretaker to direct her to Mr. LeBlanc's grave. Once she found it, she knelt down on the damp earth and cried for Mary/Joseph, her son (she always thought of him as her son) who would never run through fall leaves, never play marbles in the warm spring mud, never hug a puppy, never call her Mother. Then, recalling the tiny little blue velvet box that Sister Cordelia had shown her, she fretted in case God may not have noticed that there was a second soul in Mr. LeBlanc's casket. It was such a small case, she reasoned. God could easily overlook it, and if He did, that would mean Mary/Joseph would forever be floating around in the sky, like a rocket out of its orbit.

Laura consoled herself by saying that, surely, if He could see a little brown sparrow dropping into a wheat field in Saskatchewan or Manitoba, He would have no chance of missing an indigo blue velvet box floating around in the sky. Before she stood up, she removed her Fredericton High School ring from her little finger. Because her flesh was still carrying weight from her pregnancy, she had to ease the ring off her swollen finger by moistening finger and ring with her tongue. She then burrowed a hole in the soft clay, just slightly off from the center of the grave (she liked to believe that the undertaker had tucked Mary/Joseph in Mr. LeBlanc's breast pocket), and then she dropped in the ring. Now Mary/Joseph would have something to remember her by, and something familiar for him to hold onto in the dark. Just before turning to leave, she thanked Mr. LeBlanc for taking her child into eternity. Although she was certain Mr. LeBlanc could understand English as well as she could, as a special courtesy she resurrected words from her high school French and offered her thanks to him in that language.

By the time her mother came to pick her up to take her to Halifax, Laura was back in the hospital waiting room ready to leave. She said nothing about her excursion to Mary/Joseph's grave. Mrs. MacPhail helped her into the car, wrapped a blanket around her and told her that she had to take it easy for awhile in order to get her strength back and go on with her life.

The problem was that Laura didn't see much of a life to go on with, especially after she arrived in Halifax. The apartment Kevin had rented for them was in an older home near the city center, on Sally Street. They had the downstairs flat and a young man, a graduate student in Kevin's faculty named Jesse Morris, had the upper flat. Actually, it was through Jesse that Kevin had heard about the vacant flat.

The flat was cobbled together, it was dreary and drafty, and it had stale breath, as if cigar smokers had been the previous tenants. To Laura, the whole place presented a sharp contrast to her mother's bright, fresh-smelling, colour-coordinated home and she wished she were back again in her lavendar rose bedroom. The walls in every room — even in the kitchen — had been updated with brown wall-board. The windows were long and narrow, and what light they let in was eaten up by the brown boards. As it turned out, even in the middle of the day she had to keep a lamp on in every room.

The day Laura and her mother arrived at the flat, Kevin was still at the university but he had left a note in an envelope pinned to the porch curtain. It said that the key could be located underneath the rope mat on the entrance step. Both Laura and her mother carefully avoided comment as they walked through the flat, taking stock of warped doors that wouldn't close, uneven floors that were covered with worn carpet, and kitchen appliances that once upon a time had been white but were now yellowed with age. Although Laura had never fantasized about a Betty Crocker kitchen complete with gleaming counters and geraniums on the window-sill, and she had never lusted for hardwood floors or furniture saturated in Pledge, this flat and its furnishings fell well below her expectations. And she knew it certainly fell well below her mother's. She could tell this by her mother's silent, down-turned mouth. When they entered the kitchen, neither of them commented on the unwashed dishes on the table, in the sink and on the stove. Neither did they comment on another note of Kevin's — the one on the kitchen sink apologizing for the mess, saying he hadn't had time to "detail" the place but he would help out when he got back.

Mrs. MacPhail, who had booked a hotel for overnight because she intended to take up no more of her daughter's privacy than necessary, immediately announced that she was going to spend an extra night in Halifax to help Laura "get settled" — her way of saying that she couldn't possibly leave her just-released-from-the-hospital daughter in such dire straits. After she made up the bed with fresh linen and tucked Laura into it, she tackled the kitchen.

Laura often wondered how her mother had described the flat to her father because within a week a cheque arrived with the instructions that it was to help Laura and Kevin make the place a little more livable. Along with the cheque, there was a pointed remark that Laura should take good care of herself, as she had been through an ordeal and needed all the rest she could get.

But Laura soon found that rest was the least of her needs. She had plenty of time for rest — indeed, far too much time. Kevin was at the university from early morning until late at night, and when he came home he was usually so tired he went to bed immediately. He hardly had enough energy to say good night to her, much less carry on a conversation. But she didn't blame him for this; she had grown up in an academic environment and she knew the demands on a first-year professor, especially one who was still in the process of finishing his dissertation. Still, understanding Kevin's shortage of time didn't make her empty hours any easier to bear. Indeed, she soon became so severely lonely that during the daylight hours she found herself peeking around the living-room curtains at the small signs of life on her street — neighbours talking across lawns, the mailman trudging up the sidewalk, old women walking their dogs at precisely the same time each day, students going to the little store on the corner and returning with snacks.

In fact, she spent so much time looking at these small dregs of life that took place on the other side of her living-room window that she felt she knew her neighbours, even though she had never met them. For instance, she knew that the tidily dressed, blue-haired woman who lived across the street had a cleaning lady come in every Tuesday morning, and that just before this person came to clean, the blue-haired woman, with a scarf protecting her hair, would bustle around inside her house, straightening up the living room — even shaking out the mat she kept in her foyer. And Laura knew that the young woman who also lived across the street, two houses down — and whose house was much like

Laura's own, a house converted into flats — was divorced and had two school-aged children. Laura surmised that the young mother worked in a doctor's office because she left home every morning at the same time, but returned at staggered times in the evening. And she always wore a white fortrel or polyester uniform that allowed her pink slip to show through. Every second Friday evening, shortly after this woman got home from work, her ex-husband would pull into her driveway to collect the children. As the man bustled about, settling the children into the car, the woman would always stand back from her window, out of his line of vision, and size him up. Just as soon as he left she would go for a walk, still in her uniform — as if she couldn't bear to be alone in the house, not even long enough to change clothes.

Laura felt an instant kinship with this young woman. She imagined her loneliness, imagined her aborted dreams, imagined her walking through the weekend-empty house recalling the numerous times she had plumped up her husband's ego, given substance to his sentences, soothed his hurts, and all to no avail, all her efforts having ended in watching him drive away with her children, probably taking them home to his lover. Seeing the woman's actions, and sensing her pain, made Laura wonder whether she would ever brood over a man that much, whether she would ever brood over Kevin to that extent. With such thoughts she always came away from the window, promising herself that as soon as she had enough energy, she would try and make friends with this woman because it probably would do both of them the world of good.

As her mother had advised, she made certain to take care of herself, but no matter how much time she spent on the couch, no matter how long she stayed in bed, no matter how much sleep she got, her weariness never went away. She always felt as limp and as droopy as the velour drapes on the living-room window. Each morning she would will herself to get up, hoping that a surge of energy from somewhere would course through her body so that this day would be a better one than the day before.

Finally, after several weeks of total lethargy, and at her

mother's telephoned insistence, she went to a doctor. But, other than learning that her exhaustion was due to post-partum depression, the trip was a waste of time. The doctor told her to get interested in something outside the home, to put the miscarriage behind her, to make new friends. But she had barely enough energy to listen to his advice, much less act upon it.

Kevin parroted the doctor's advice. He was at a loss as to what else he could do. Sometimes he tried to spend more time with Laura in the evenings, but she was always aware it was borrowed time. At such times he would tell her stories from his classes, from his labs, from his office. They were humorous stories and she would force herself to laugh out loud, as he intended her to do. On those evenings, after they went to bed, she would feel a sudden rush of physical need and she would say to Kevin, "Hold me. I need to feel loved." He would always oblige by putting his arms around her. Once in a while, after the doctor said it was safe to do so, they even made love. On the mornings following the lovemaking, she always had a brighter outlook and she would be certain that she was well on her way to getting her health back.

Other times, though, Kevin became impatient with her, asking when she was going to snap out of "it." He said "it" as if she were languishing on the couch like a Victorian lady with the vapours. Once, when Jesse Morris — the graduate student who lived above them — came down to visit, Kevin remarked in an aside to her (although she was sure Jesse heard him) that she looked like an unmade bed with her mismatched skirt and blouse, and slippers that looked like dustmops. They made love that night as well — Kevin's way of making amends — but the next morning she still felt dispirited, so much so that she faced him down and asked him why he had insulted her in front of company.

"That's precisely why I said what I said," he explained, by way of apology. "I was embarrassed in front of Jesse. No man wants his wife to look like a dustmop in front of his friends. Besides, I whispered, so you're the only one who heard."

Unbeknownst to her at the time, that first visit of Jesse's began a pattern of nightly visits. Jesse came downstairs as regularly as clockwork, as soon as Kevin got home from the university. Even though it angered Laura that Jesse's visits cut so severely into her time with Kevin, she was determined never to shame Kevin again when Jesse was present. Indeed, she summoned all of her energy and made a point of dressing more carefully for those times when she knew Jesse would see her. To her surprise, after a few weeks it didn't seem to be such an effort anymore and one day she felt sprightly enough to go downtown to a dress shop, where she splurged on a new skirt and sweater. The money came from a cheque her mother had sent her, along with a brief note in her mother's careful writing stating that this cheque was hers and hers alone. She was to consider it "mad money." Under the circumstances, Laura thought that was an inappropriate phrase, but she knew no harm had been meant by it.

When Jesse next visited, she knew she looked her best, yet instead of complimenting her, he seemed jealous of her new vitality. He said she was too thin and too pale.

"What's wrong with that fellow?" she demanded of Kevin as soon as Jesse left. "He's as mean-spirited as a weasel. And I'm getting sick and tired of him always hanging out here. He seems to resent my presence. As if I have no right to be here."

Her words started the first real fight between the two of them.

"Can't you understand that we have a lot in common," Kevin snapped, as if she were attacking him instead of Jesse. "We don't have time during the day to talk things over. I can't see what's wrong with being able to relax and talk to someone in your field after your day's work is over." He peered at her intently over his reading glasses, as if he were sizing up her sanity. "And why should he resent you anyway?" When she had no answer, he went back to browsing through the recently released examination schedule, mumbling to himself something she was supposed to hear — something about getting a grip on her life.

A few minutes later, as if something in the examination schedule had triggered a definitive response to her criticism of Jesse's visits, he came out to the kitchen where she was clearing up the last of the supper dishes and said to her that it seemed unreasonable that it was all right for her to go across the street and visit with Frances, the dentist's receptionist, with whom she seemed to have become fast friends, but that it wasn't all right for him to have a colleague visit him in his own living room. When Laura tried to explain that she never visited Frances when Kevin was at home to keep her company, her explanation sounded as lame to her as it must have to Kevin. So she apologized and admitted she was just being selfish, and asked him to ignore what she had just said about Jesse.

But her outburst had served to bring about a small change for the better. Jesse didn't visit as often. Still, whenever he did, he managed to irritate her. And, of course, he always did this in ways Kevin didn't notice. Once he came down wearing one of Kevin's white tee-shirts, and he called attention to this fact by pointing to an indelible pen mark underneath the pocket flap. He waited until he caught her eye and then, in a falsely innocent voice, said, "I seem to have stubbed my pen on my pocket. But at least it's out of sight." Then he said, dismissively, as if he had a thousand other things on his mind that were more important than an ink blot on his shirt, "I can't remember ever using an idelible pen when I had this shirt on. Of course, it may not even be mine. Perhaps I picked up someone else's shirt by mistake at the swimming pool or the gym."

Laura knew Jesse was wearing Kevin's shirt. More importantly, Jesse knew she knew. The previous week she had gone out and bought new clothes for Kevin with another sum of money her mother had sent. When she had removed the tags from his tee-shirt, a spot of wet indelible ink that had lain unnoticed on her thumbnail — ink that was left over from a leaky pen she had used when she was making up garage sale posters for Frances — had spotted the underflap of the shirt pocket and no amount of washing would remove it.

"How come Jesse is wearing the shirt I bought you?" she demanded of Kevin a few days later, after the incident had simmered and soured inside her and after she had searched his bureau drawer and the laundry basket for the errant tee-shirt.

"Who says he's wearing my tee-shirt?" Kevin countered, his tone long-suffering, as if he was now going to be subjected to still another inquisition session. He shook his head as if her question bemused him. "How can you tell one white tee-shirt from another, anyway?"

"Because yours had an ink spot on the pocket. That's how," she shot back. "An indelible ink spot. Underneath the flap."

Without showing the slightest sign of being nonplussed, Kevin offered an easy, off-hand explanation. "If it's mine, perhaps he picked it up by mistake in one of the locker rooms at the gym, or at the swimming pool. We go there at the same time. Both facilities are open for faculty and graduates between eleven-thirty and twelve-thirty. And the place is littered with white tee-shirts." He added for extra support, "And, anyway, who says it's mine. Other people besides you are in possession of indelible ink pens."

Laura merely shrugged and let the subject drop, but she knew it was Kevin's tee-shirt. Just as a mother cat knows her own kittens from another cat's kittens, she knew her husband's clothes. But the explanation as to how Jesse had got hold of the shirt sounded plausible and innocent enough, so she went on to something else.

What angered her about Jesse having the shirt was her stubborn belief that Kevin had given it to him — a shirt that had been bought out of her mother's gift money, out of money she could have spent on herself. She never brought up the subject again, even though on several occasions Jesse wore the shirt in her presence. She just made up her mind that a tee-shirt wasn't worth spoiling the few hours she had with Kevin each day.

S i x

Laura tugs at the neck of her green tee-shirt, hauling it down to give her skin some air. "I've had it, Hannah," she says, veering the car into the parking lot of a roadside restaurant on the outskirts of Edmundston. "Especially with that sun. It's all yours after lunch." She tosses the keys to Hannah, saying, "I'm starved. I hope there's something good on the menu." Together they get out of the car and walk across the parking lot towards the restaurant.

As they wait for a waitress they complain about how boring the drive is from Fredericton to Quebec City, and how Laura dreads the repeat journey in the morning. They discuss the lack of choice on the menu and lament that they didn't choose a different restaurant — one that served more salads. The conversation is innocuous, but civil. When Hannah brings up the subject of Laura and Kevin's marriage, the talk clings safely to the margins. They discuss who attended the wedding, what Laura's mother wore, where they lived in Halifax, and on and on, until Hannah, who still needs a more thorough scavaging of her parents' marriage in order to make sense of its disintegration, asks, "Did you blame Dad for losing the baby?" Some of the old surliness surfaces in her voice.

Laura shakes her head emphatically. "No. How could I? It wasn't his fault. It was nobody's fault."

"But if he had stayed in Fredericton for the night. If ..."

Laura toys with her fork for a few seconds before shaking her head again. "I never asked him to stay in Fredericton. I had no idea

I was going to miscarry. Besides it wouldn't have mattered. The doctor said as much."

She puckers her forehead, remembering that it wasn't where the miscarriage had taken place that had troubled her, but how Kevin had reacted to it. She offers this to Hannah. "What bothered me the most about the miscarriage was that I didn't think your father took it very hard. He didn't seem to understand that for me it was like losing a full-term child. It wasn't just a fetus, as he insisted on calling it — something to be pulled out and thrown away like a fingernail you had smashed with a hammer. But that's how he thought. And I blamed him for that. Rightly or wrongly."

Laura shrugs, absolving Kevin for calling Mary/Joseph an expelled fetus. "Maybe it's a woman thing and most men wouldn't understand, not just your father. But at the time, I resented him for that. I just didn't have a lot of experience with such things. And I certainly wasn't prepared for the depression that landed on me within a few days and just kept on and on and on."

She describes to Hannah how she went into an extended post-partum depression after her mother returned to Fredericton and she was left alone day after day in the dreary flat.

"The doctor said that depression sometimes happens after miscarriages as well as after full-term pregnancies. Mine lasted for months. Actually, the best part of a year." She gives a half laugh. "There used to be a character in a comic strip who went around with a cloud over his head. I think his name was *Pfffft* or something like that. Anyway, that's how I felt all the time. As if there was no colour in the world. Just this grey weight on my shoulders." She looks off across the restaurant, remembering. "It was awful," she confesses. "At first your father was very considerate, but I think his patience wore thin after awhile. He thought I should have snapped out of it. Especially since it wasn't a *real* child." Laura makes this last remark in a voice that is supposed to mimic Kevin's, and adds, her tone cynical, "As if my body chemistry knew the difference."

She then hurries to Kevin's defense, to forestall Hannah's defense of him. "But to give him his due, he was really worried. I

86

think that's why he was willing to move back to Fredericton after you were born. He was afraid the depression would start up again. And at least I had friends in Fredericton and I wouldn't be so much alone." She shrugs. "But of course it wasn't about being away from Fredericton. Or about being alone. It was a chemical upset that would have happened even if I had never left Fredericton. Or even if I had been in the midst of friends twenty-four hours a day."

Hannah is even more confused than before. She asks point blank the question that earlier she had skirted. "If you and Dad only got married because you were pregnant, why didn't you divorce sooner — right after the miscarriage? Why wait till now?"

Laura gives reasons that had made sense twenty years earlier. "There was my depression," she states flatly, as though that would be reason enough in itself. "And, of course, divorce wasn't so common then. It would have been a big disgrace, especially in Granpy and Grandma's eyes. And your father was just getting a foothold in his work. He was putting the better part of his energy into that. And then I was pregnant again ... and ..." She tosses her hands in the air, not expecting a woman of the '90s to understand why a woman of an earlier generation had settled for less than the Grand Passion, or less than total fulfilment.

"We made a nice couple," she says, as if this fact in itself is an explanation. "I was a regular Susie Homemaker. Your father had his work. And then there was you. It seemed to be enough until ..."

Too late, Laura realizes she has talked herself into a trap and has left herself open for Hannah to ask, "until what?" She quickly reaches for the menu, hoping to change the subject. "Let's order," she says edgily, beckoning the waitress.

They both order the same meal — double decker sandwiches — but no sooner is the order placed than Hannah turns back to where they had left off, pressing for answers that will help her make sense out of the marriage break-up. She not only asks the question Laura had hoped she wouldn't ask, she goes on to list the reasons why she is so bewildered by what is happening in the family.

"Until what?" she prods. "Until the artist came along?" Because she still feels the need to mangle Claude's name, she omits it. "What brought it all to a head now?" She hurries with affirmations in support of her father, as if, despite what has been said, she still thinks it is Laura who solely and singly initiated the break-up. "You can't tell me Dad wasn't good to you. I remember him giving you Neo Citran whenever you had a cold. And he always looked after your car. Took it to the garage and all."

The waitress brings the sandwiches. For the moment, Hannah ignores her food and continues to list reasons why the marriage should remain intact. "And you didn't fight. Not like Sally's parents. They're always fighting about something. Stupid things. Like whether the *Gleaner* comes out before noon or in the afternoon on Saturday. Or whether there was snow on the ground last Christmas Eve. They're always picking away at each other. It can really get on your nerves."

While Laura listens she reorganizes her sandwich, removing the bacon she had forgotten to tell the waitress to hold. That was one thing Kevin had never understood about her — why she wouldn't eat the flesh of animals. She once told him that she'd eat meat if he could convince her that it had never covered the heart of an animal — that it originated in neat cellophane packages in the deep freeze section of the supermarket.

She pops a piece of tomato into her mouth. "You know, Hannah," she says, pausing for a second to swallow the tomato wedge so that she can talk without sounding guttural. "You keep heaping the responsibility for the failure of the marriage on me. As if I'm the only one who wants out. And you also seem to think that because your father and I are usually civil to one another, there's nothing basically wrong with the marriage."

Then, as if reconsidering what she has just said, she adds, "Maybe it's just that we're not the type of people who are always rowing with each other. That doesn't mean we didn't have a gutful of anger from time to time." She starts to say that maybe there wasn't enough passion to make fighting worthwhile, but realizes that would only confuse Hannah further. She says instead, "Maybe we didn't row with each other because we loved you enough to want to give you a peaceful home."

Laura fully expects Hannah to make a testy remark about trying to lay a guilt trip on her. Much to her surprise, Hannah makes no comment whatsoever. To Laura, this silence is even more unsettling than Hannah's earlier churlishness. However, Laura soon realizes that Hannah hasn't responded because she has been backtracking through the years, looking for signs of discord she might have missed or might have been led to miss.

"Parents should be more honest with children," Hannah says, obviously unable to find signs of discord sufficient to destroy a marriage, and feeling she had the right to be allowed to see these signs if they had existed. "They shouldn't hide things from their kids."

In hindsight, Laura tends to agree, but before she has a chance to say so, Hannah startles her with a question. Although there is a challenge in her tone, her words come out weak and hesitant, as if there is only one answer her ears can bear to hear. "But I was planned, wasn't I? Not just an accident like Mary/Joseph?"

"You were a much wanted child. Very much wanted," Laura supplies quickly by way of evasion. She can't very well tell Hannah that her father and mother had made love so seldom that a pregnancy could not be planned; nor can she say that Hannah's presence in this world is due to a random act of intercourse, a hit or miss conception, a night when the moon and stars and Kevin were all in harmony.

She elaborates on how much Hannah was wanted by stating that her pregnancy and birth coincided with one of the more satisfying periods in Laura and Kevin's marriage. She acknowledges that, at first, Kevin was tentative about being a father, and had some misgivings about the pregnancy. He was fearful about the extent to which it would curb his life. She admits, too, that at first she had misgivings. She would have liked to have returned to university. But, as the months passed, and Kevin began spending more and more time at home and she began feeling life inside her, things changed for the better: Kevin lost his tentativeness and she lost her misgivings.

Laura adds that Kevin was so anxious that his child have the best of everything, he even reluctantly accepted money from Laura's parents for a more upscale apartment for them. She tells Hannah how happy she was to move away from Sally Street, but omits the part about being glad that she was no longer a neighbour of Jesse Morris'. She does tell her that she still lived close enough to Sally Street to visit her new-found friend, Frances, and that on Frances' afternoon off from her dentist office job they often went to a movie together.

Laura recalls how, when Hannah was born, Kevin was completely overwhelmed with fatherhood. He came to her bedside the morning after the birth and, as he held her hand very tenderly, said, "Thank you for giving me the most beautiful little girl in the world." She had heard that new mothers have a glow about them and she believed it at that moment because she felt a joyous heat flooding her body and flushing her cheeks and making her eyes sparkle.

Jesse, of whom she had seen very little during her pregnancy, especially towards the end, visited their new home after she came out of the hospital. Although he supposedly came to see Hannah, he paid no attention to her whatsoever, just gave her an obligatory look and then started talking to Kevin about work. After he left, Laura mentioned casually to Kevin that Jesse seemed to be jealous of Hannah because he had deliberately ignored her. Instead of huffily denying her assertion, as she expected, Kevin walked over to Hannah's crib and stared down at the sleeping child. His face took on a gentleness she had never witnessed before. "Who wouldn't be jealous of such a beautiful daughter," he said, bending down to touch Hannah's downy soft face with the tips of his fingers.

Laura had wanted to say, "I know what you mean. I'm even a little jealous of her myself." She remembered an earlier time when they were living on Sally Street. She had said something similar to Kevin — about Jesse resenting her own time with Kevin, and he had laughed and tossed away her observation, saying, "Where do you get such nonsense from, Laura?" She has always wished he had said, "Who wouldn't be jealous of such a beautiful wife."

While Laura sits in the restaurant, she cuts and snips these memories — not willy-nilly, but with much deliberation — and gives them to Hannah, again omitting the part about Jesse, but admitting that she felt a twinge of envy whenever Kevin acted as though he had manufactured all by himself the most beautiful child in the world. But she admits her envy in a mocking, self-deprecatory way so that Hannah's set mouth breaks into a satisfied smile, finding herself able to abide her mother's jealousy in the satiety of her father's intemperate love.

While Hannah, always a slow, picky eater, finishes her sandwich, Laura sips her coffee and remembers how the marriage settled itself into studied civility, strictly for Hannah's sake, and how this civility continued year in and year out long after all signs of passion had passed — or, more specifically, long after Laura knew that there never had been any signs of passion to pass. She recalls how she and Kevin would sit on the sofa in the evenings, surrounded by small talk that was mostly about domestic things: Hannah's grades and whether the child would be exempted from writing examinations again this year; the cat's litter box and whether it was time to move it out of the basement for another season; whether the house could use a fresh coat of paint. But their real conversations were always carried on in long patches of silence. Her silence — the empty place in her heart — was always filled with the same question: If he had the choice, would Kevin be sitting here with her now? Was he here because it was not convenient for him to be there? However, she was never certain where there was. And always in the back reaches of her mind were other questions: Am I expecting too much of marriage? Is this all there is to it? Is this what marriage is — two people sharing a roof, sharing a child and little else.

Eventually the silences and the empty spaces in their hearts exacted a toll and the two of them found ways to hold out on each other. This was not done with malice aforethought, and not in any public way, and certainly not in any way that Hannah would notice. It was as if, subconsciously, they each came to the realization that if they gave less, they would hurt less.

They held out on the little things — things that weren't easily noticed but that bind lives together in love. Laura, for example, continued to give Kevin the obligatory birthday and Christmas and Father's Day presents — the shirt and tie, the sweater, the pen and pencil set — but she withheld the special cologne that, in the early days, she used to order from Montreal. And she continued to give Kevin good quality socks, but she withheld the saucy underwear. And towards the very end, she stopped making him "from scratch" birthday cakes. She just bought the supermarket cakes with the sickly sweet icing and blue roses — those "one size fits all" cakes where the salesclerk simply had to squeeze Kevin's name from a funnel filled with runny icing.

But in depriving Kevin, Laura also deprived herself. She became less lighthearted, less joyful, less giving. During the later years of her marriage, if anyone had asked her to draw a picture of herself, she would have drawn a spare woman with a puckered mouth and with eyes that reflected the stinginess of her life, the desolation of it.

On Kevin's part, he never gave Laura flowers spontaneously, although he always remembered them on her birthday and Mother's Day. And when he bought these obligatory gifts, they were always store wrapped, in common-looking paper from one of those big rolls. And they were always topped with a bow the clerk had made from skinny ribbon. And what plundered her being the most — what leached away her soul — was not the store bought presents, nor the cheap, hurried-up wrappings. It was that Kevin never seemed to notice that she held out on him emotionally. He would get Hannah to help him blow out the candles on the ready-made cake, just as if it had been a cake she had spent all day making. And they would both laugh when all the candles were doused in a single blow.

Of course, Laura would laugh too, for Hannah's sake — a thin, superficial laugh, that was barely thick enough to keep her pain from being visible. She would watch Kevin cut the dry crumbly cake and she would wish that he had made love to her the night before when she had moved close to him and put her arms around his neck. Or even that he had turned towards her and allowed her to curve her cheek into the hollow of his throat, while his broad hand had smoothed her hair. And she would be wishing she had been able to make him a cake from scratch.

When Laura and Hannah leave the restaurant and go to the car, Hannah settles herself easily into the driver's seat. The food and the talk have mellowed her. She laughs out loud when, as soon as they pull out on the highway, she sees just ahead of them the van with "Bell" on its side.

"Will you look at that," she says, her sulleness all but dissipated. "There goes our Bell friend." She shakes her head, perplexed. "I don't understand how we can keep passing him unless he stops when we stop. And even at that he must get the jump on us after each stop."

Laura notices that Hannah's mood has lifted and she dares to be teasing. "When he stops for gas he doesn't spend as long in the bathroom untangling his hair as you do."

"Hardly," Laura declares archly, although not offensively. "Look at him when we go by. He looks like a skinhead."

Hannah leans her foot on the gas pedal and pulls around the truck. As she does so, Laura waves to the driver.

Hannah is appalled. "I can't believe you did that, Mother!" she says, taking her hand from the wheel to brush her wind-tossed hair away from her face. "You'd never let *me* do that. You'd say I was taunting him to chase us. Or worse."

Laura, who can still feel Hannah's earlier tentative touch on her arm, answers lightly, "I just felt like doing that. It's such a nice day. I just wanted to share it."

They fall into silence for the next couple of miles, but the silence is no longer off-putting. After several minutes, Hannah breaks the quiet and surprises Laura by recalling an incident from when Laura was a young mother.

"You know what you reminded me of back there? When you waved at the trucker? It reminded me of the time when I was about five and a bunch of us little kids were up in that linden tree beside our house and a group of you mothers were walking along the sidewalk. You had been into Cindy Smith's house for coffee."

"I remember that time," Laura cuts in, laughing. "The mothers were terrified that their little darlings were going to fall out of the tree and break something and they were shocked at me because …"

Hannah interrupts and finishes, "… Because you said, 'Don't stop now, Hannah. One more branch and you'll be at the top.' And you climbed up yourself and we both pretended we were Jack in the Bean Stalk and we sat there and looked out over the city." She confides, some of the excitement of that day now surfacing in her voice, "It was like I was doing something naughty, but it was all right because you said it was all right."

Once more they drop into silence, each one mentally reliving that occasion. Again, it is Hannah who speaks first, and once more she surprises Laura.

"When I think back, I remember there were times when you used to be a lot of fun when I was a little kid. It was mostly when Dad was away. I remember one time at Hallowe'en. Dad was out of town and we were alone. I was just getting over the chickenpox and you didn't want me out trick-or-treating because it was a cold night, so I stayed in and you dressed the both of us as monsters. We dragged those chains after us — the ones you found in the garage — when we'd answer the door and the kids would take off in fright and we'd have to call them back." She laughs, recalling the terrified looks on the faces of the neighbourhood children.

But her laugh quickly peters out, and her lips tighten flat. She looks squarely at Laura and says wistfully, "I wish you'd stayed that way all the time." She says this as if Laura had deliberately sabotaged all whimsy and airiness in her spirit. "Most of the time you were so long-faced. And the older I got, the longer-faced you got. I always had this queasy feeling that you didn't want to be around Dad and me. That you didn't like us. But I'd hear you talking on the phone and you'd be laughing. And one time I met some of your students at a basketball tournament and they all liked you." She looks baffled. "I don't understand how you could be so different with them. With us you always looked like ... I don't know ... like, well, like we turned you sour or something. That you couldn't stand being around us."

Laura shakes her head in quick denial, appalled that Hannah would have perceived her this way. "That's not true," she says adamantly. "I mean, it's not true that I didn't want to be around you. Or that I didn't like you. Love you, for that matter. There's never been a moment when that hasn't been true." She lets the "you" stand for whomever Hannah wants it to stand for. Then, aware she's not speaking the whole truth, she amends. "Well, if we're setting the record straight you should know there's two sides to this story. Perhaps you should recall that if I got more long-faced with the years, you certainly got harder to deal with, too. And the older you got, the more you sided with your father, and the more you pushed me to the fringes of your life." She stops, takes a deep breath and then plunges onward. "So, to be blunt with you, there were times when it wasn't all fun and games having you in my life. Sometimes I even found myself tallying up the good days and the bad days to see if it was all worth it, and whether I'd do it over again if I had the choice."

The remark triggers Hannah's belligerence. "Is that why you were going to leave home this spring? You thought Dad and I weren't worth it?"

Laura is shocked. "What? I've no idea what you're talking about."

Hannah gives Laura a "Don't try and pull that innocent stuff on me" look, and her voice reverts to its scalding tone of the morning. "Oh, you know what I'm talking about all right."

But then, just in case, she jogs Laura's memory so that she won't be able to use forgetfulness as a feigned excuse. "Remember the day I came in the house and you and Dad were in the bedroom? It was around the end of May. You two must have had a real bad argument or something because Dad said, 'You can't leave, Laura.

95

You have to stay for Hannah's sake.' He had to beg you to stay."
She gives Laura a quick, scorching look. "And don't try to fudge
and say I was hearing things. I know what I heard."

To Hannah's surprise, Laura makes no attempt at defense.
"I'm not going to fudge. I remember that day. It was this May. Late
May. I just didn't ... we didn't ... neither of us realized you had
overheard. You never said anything. I remember you were at
school and you just came in and went into your bedroom to phone
someone."

Hannah cuts to the point, her words blunt. She doesn't bother
to say that she overheard other bits and pieces of that argument, none
of which made any sense to her then, but all of which she has quietly
hoarded and all of which she blames on Laura.

"Was that artist fellow around then?" As if those other
moments — those companionable moments in the car — have
been obliterated, she adds, her tone scathing and her accusing
words straining the fragile connection that has so tenuously been
formed between them, "Or was it another artist?"

Laura sucks in her breath. It is a sudden, small gasp of hurt,
but she speaks tightly, determined not to fuel the moment. "There
was no one around for me. Artist or otherwise."

"Then why were you leaving?" Hannah doesn't wait for
Laura's answer but gives her own. "Now I s'pose you're going to
tell me there was someone around for Dad?"

Just in case that is Laura's intention, Hannah builds up a
quick defence for her father. "I s'pose some woman looked at him
sideways and you got bent out of shape thinking he was having an
affair."

She lists reasons why she would expect her mother to do such
a thing. "You were jealous of Dad, that was it, wasn't it? You were
always jealous of any one who paid him attention. Even me." She
goes on to jog Laura's memory about the statement she made
earlier. "Remember back a few minutes ago, you said you were
envious when Dad used to crow over me when I was a baby. I
believe you. You were always jealous because he and I were so
close. I could feel it. Especially when I'd ask Dad to come watch

me skate. I never asked you because you were always busy getting supper or doing something around the house. That's the only reason. Besides, you don't like the cold."

She changes her tack. "But it wasn't just me you were jealous of. You were jealous of Dad's graduate students and colleagues, especially Jesse Morris." She says this in a belittling tone, wanting the argument she overheard to be about a trivial matter. "That day of the argument, when you were going to leave, did Jesse phone or something? I know his closeness to Dad irritated you enough to get you that roiled up. He must've called from Halifax because I heard Dad say his name. He said something like 'Don't blame Jesse. Blame me.' Is that what made you blow your cool?"

Worried that Hannah is getting too close to the truth, Laura confesses just enough truth to rein her in. "Your father lied to me and I caught him in the lie. That's what the argument was about. And I'm not going to say anymore. It's between the two of us and not your concern."

"Something to do with Jesse Morris?"

When Laura neither denies nor assents, Hannah is sure she has detected the cause of the argument. She cuts and splices the information she possesses and makes it into something she can grab onto. "You were jealous because Dad was with him on the trip. They travelled together to the Learneds Conference. That's it, isn't it? I remember how you used to say he took up too much of Dad's time. And Dad would say that Jesse was a colleague, that their work was in the same field. They had to collaborate, and he asked you to understand that. But you'd pull your face down whenever he called. You never said too much, but the twist of your mouth said it all."

In her renewed annoyance with her mother, Hannah extends her information. "And Jesse knew how you felt, too. And he thought you were being ridiculous. I remember one time when I was about eight and Jesse was on his way back to Halifax. He and Dad had gone to a conference somewhere."

"That was also a Learneds Conference. It was May," Laura contributes, remembering very well whenever Jesse's presence had crossed her life, and not bothering to negate Hannah's perception of her as an unreasonable woman. It would only be wasting her breath.

"Whatever," Hannah says, impatient at quibbling over such an irrelevant detail. It reminds her of her friend's father and mother fighting over the *Gleaner*.

"And Dad was taking me to swimming lessons and he swung by the Beaverbrook Hotel to pick up Jesse and take him somewhere or other. To the airport, I think. I was in the back seat. They were talking back and forth — something about you being jealous of him. Jesse was laughing at you."

Hannah looks at Laura, expecting her to reply. When she doesn't, Hannah prompts, "That proves you were jealous of everyone who had anything to do with Dad, doesn't it?"

Laura doesn't reply because she is totally enveloped in picturing Jesse and Kevin together, and Jesse laughing at her. And Kevin not taking her part. In front of Hannah! The thought of the two of them conspiring against her, ridiculing her in front of Hannah, bloats her body with so much pain that it is impossible for her frame to contain it, so it shoots up her neck and jaws looking for a way out. But because the pain can't find any way out, it starts to twist into what she knows is the beginning of a migraine. She forages in her purse on the pretext of looking for a breath mint, and extracts two double strength Tylenol. She pops them into her mouth and swallows them dry. They lodge in her throat.

Because Hannah is still waiting for an answer, Laura supplies one. "I had my reasons for disliking Jesse Morris." Her words are taut, allowing no slack, so that Hannah will know for certain the subject will not be elaborated upon. "I still have my reasons, for that matter. But they're staying my reasons."

Hannah will not be put off so easily. Her fingers tighten on the wheel and she angrily pulls out around the slow-moving traffic, as if it is the traffic that is offending her. Hoping to goad Laura into giving more details, she presses, "So you were jealous of anyone who took up Dad's time. That's still no reason to leave him."

Laura rubs her forehead, as if to rub away the migraine that is now making inroads towards the top of her head. She wonders whether taking the Tylenol dry will prevent the medicine's absorbtion into her system. If it does, she will soon be sick to her stomach. She reflects that Hannah doesn't know what embarrassment is until she sees her mother on the side of the highway vomiting up a migraine.

She says, almost fretfully, "Hannah, can't you accept that your father and I are not suited to each other and let it go at that? Were never suited to each other. Can't you accept that it's his choice to end this marriage just as much as it's mine? Can't you accept that it has nothing to do with people outside of our marriage? And especially that it has nothing to do with you?"

To hammer home this last part, Laura rubs the back of her neck to push off the pain and says, "You were then, and always will be, first in our hearts. That's something I want you never to forget. Even during those times you didn't ask me to go skating with you, I would have given my life for you. And you know very well your father would have done the same."

S e v e n

Hannah was born in the spring of 1969, two years and a few weeks after Laura's miscarriage. Shortly after the birth, and as soon as the university semester was over, Kevin and Laura moved back to Fredericton. Professor MacPhail had decided to take early retirement and move home to Vancouver. One of his last "calling in of markers" was to get a spot in his faculty for his son-in-law. When that was accomplished, he sold Kevin his house in Fredericton for a miniscule sum because nothing was too good or too much for his one and only grandchild.

When Laura was first presented with the news that they would be returning to Fredericton and to her parents' house, she felt so much joy she was sure that at that moment she had received her lifetime's measure of happiness all in one fell swoop. She could picture Hannah in the bedroom that had once been her own, with the lavendar rose walls and curtains changed to something more suitable for a nursery. She could see Hannah playing in the big back yard underneath the maples and birches, and climbing up those trees and racing squirrels to the top.

Immediately on the heels of this good news, Kevin tarnished her joy by announcing that Jesse Morris would be going to Fredericton as well. "What business has he got going there, just because we're going?" she asked, not caring that Kevin always made it quite plain he hated small-minded people who only cared about their own interests. "What business does he have to chase after us?"

Kevin took great pains to explain to her why Jesse was going to Fredericton, and his willingness to explain told Laura that he was delighted that Jesse would be tagging along. He said that Jesse had completed his Masters degree and now he wanted to get his Doctorate, but that he didn't think it was wise to get two advanced degrees from the same university. "He'll be in Fredericton for about three years," Kevin said. "And he's even been offered a position back here when he's finished."

"Let him go somewhere else," Laura threw out scornfully. "Anyplace else." She felt inexplicably anxious. She went over and stood by Hannah's playpen, as if sensing danger for the child. She was like a cat that senses a thunderstorm brewing, and crouches low, looking for cover. She wanted to take Hannah and Kevin and hide from Jesse. "Why Fredericton? There're plenty of other universities."

"He wants to be my graduate student," Kevin told her, trying to be offhand. But by this time a small amount of trepidation had crept into his voice. It only increased Laura's own anxiety.

Kevin strained to put forth reasons why she should be glad that Jesse was going to be his graduate student. "Use your head, Laura," he rebuked her. "How many young professors take a graduate student with them when they take up a new position? And one with a large grant! It's a feather in my cap. I should think you'd be pleased for me."

But she wasn't pleased. Not at all. Yet, for the life of her, she couldn't explain why she wasn't happy. She consoled herself by remembering that she had plenty of friends in Fredericton to take up her time, so she could avoid all contact with Jesse Morris if that's what she desired. And certainly, at that moment, that's what she desired. Besides, how long could it take to get a Doctorate? Before she knew it, Jesse would be heading back to Halifax and out of her life.

The first thing Laura did after returning home to New Brunswick was drive to Moncton to visit Mary/Joseph's grave. She went on the pretext of seeing an exhibition of quilts by local craftspeople.

It was early June, and Mr. LeBlanc's grave was naked except

for a single white daisy, the seed for which had probably blown over from the surrounding pasture land. As Laura looked at the skinny little flower bending this way and that way in the raw, cold wind, she thought it looked as forlorn as Mary/Joseph must have felt when he had been left alone with a strange man in a strange city. Then she imagined the daisy being nourished by Mary/Joseph, and this thought gave her a sense of kinship with the flower. She decided to take it home where it would have the company of other daisies in the wildflower section of her father's backyard, and where she could look at it from her kitchen window and be reminded of its earlier closeness to Mary/Joseph.

With her bare fingers, Laura uprooted the flower and then wrapped it in Kleenex, which she first dampened in the dew-wet grass. As soon as she got back home, she planted it in her backyard, where it had the company of other daisies. But, for all her care in planting it, the flower never took root. A few days afterwards, before it withered completely, she snipped off its head and preserved it in glycerine.

Almost a year and a half later — it was Wednesday, the twenty-first day of October, 1970, to be exact — Laura was in her mother's kitchen. Of course, she was really in her own kitchen now, although it had taken her the best part of a year to come to think of it as such. She was in the act of coaxing a jellied lobster salad from a fish-shaped mold.

The Arts and Crafts group from the University Women's Club were coming for lunch and she had wanted to serve something a little fancier than her usual domestic fare. Hannah was taking a morning nap and Kevin was in Montreal attending a conference. He was there specifically because Jesse Morris was presenting a paper at McGill University.

The past months in Fredericton had made Laura dislike Jesse Morris even more intensely than she had when they had lived in Halifax. He was taking up entirely too much space in Kevin's life. He was always popping into the house unannounced, on the least pretext. He was more demanding than all of Kevin's other graduate students put together. And it was getting to the point where everything about the man was becoming an irritant to her. His physical appearance irritated her. He reminded her of a negative — especially during the summer months, when his yellow-blond hair was bleached almost white and his eyebrows all but disappeared into his carefully tanned face. His mannerisms irritated her. After every few sentences, he would sweep the thumb and finger of his right hand over his lips, as if rubbing away crumbs. His laugh irritated her. It had a little cough at the end of it, as though the laugh had become stuck in his throat.

Laura was certain that Jesse was aware of her feelings towards him. In fact, he played to her dislike of him by excluding her from even the simplest conversation having to do with sociology, always addressing only Kevin, just as if she wouldn't know such commonsense stuff as class structure and leadership qualities, or, for that matter, Karl Marx' ideology — the subject of Kevin's newest graduate course. One day when Jesse quoted from Marx, "From each according to his abilities, to each according to his needs," she had said scoffingly that Marx had probably cribbed this idea from the Bible — "to whom much is given, much is expected." It was the closest she had seen Jesse come to losing his cool demeanor.

"Laura," he had said with counterfeit indulgence, making her scoffing sound feeble and puny, and, as always, taking pride in his atheism, knowing it galled her. "You shouldn't mix fact with fiction. Science and religion are incompatible."

She had shot back, "On what authority can you make a statement like that, Jesse? You know nothing at all about religion."

Although she had had the last word, she had still come away from that encounter feeling a lesser person — which was the way she usually felt in Jesse's presence. Indeed, she was beginning to remind herself of the narrator in one of Browning's Monologues. Her chronic complaining about Jesse to Kevin was making her the despised one, instead of Jesse.

"You let such trifles get under your skin, Laura," Kevin told her one day, when she said to him that it was getting to the point where everything about Jesse was setting her nerves on edge, even the way he buttoned his coat — the first and the last button and then the middle one. After a short pause, as if what he was about to say was something he had hoarded for a long while, Kevin said, "Perhaps the problem lies with you, Laura — not with Jesse."

He then used Jesse's expressions to scold her, irritating her even further. "You're always so uptight. Hang loose. Jesse's brilliant. He's going to be a renowned sociologist some day. I could do a lot worse that hook my coat-tails to his star."

After that censure, Laura had tried very hard to push aside her hostility toward Jesse. But the harder she pushed, the more oppressive her dislike became. It smothered her until she could barely breathe when she was in his presence. The smothering reminded her of an incident that had occurred when she was small and had gone camping with a friend's family. It had poured rain the first night out and the tent had blown down. The soggy, linseed-oil-smelling canvas had landed on her upturned face, jolting her out of a sound sleep. She had clawed frantically at the canvas, trying to get it off her face before it choked the breath out of her. She had avoided camping ever after. But avoiding Jesse — or, for that matter, avoiding thoughts of Jesse — wasn't nearly so easy. His essence dogged her mind like a dark shadow.

Certainly, on that Wednesday morning in 1970 when she stood at her kitchen sink trying to ease the lobster salad out of its mold, Jesse's dark shadow hovered over her. He was as much with her as if he stood beside her in faded jeans and stretched-out-of-shape sweater. She had spent a lonely night tossing and turning in the queen-sized bed, her mind scudding back and forth between Jesse and Kevin, Kevin and Jesse, annoyance gathering momentum with each sleepless second. She couldn't decide which of them was more deserving of her anger, nor which of them should be anchored with her righteous indignation.

Shortly before going to bed she had telephoned Kevin to see if he was safe in his Montreal hotel. All day long the news — both on radio and television — had been flooded with developments in the FLQ crisis in Quebec. Over and over, every hour on the hour, the news had reported details of the kidnapping of Mr. Cross, the funeral of Mr. LaPorte, the introduction of martial law and the ruthlessness of the members of the FLQ, who were responsible for all of the kidnappings and other treacheries in Quebec. Because Kevin was in the midst of this upheaval, Laura had been concerned for his safety.

As she stood by the kitchen sink thinking these thoughts, Laura kept an ear cocked for the sucking sound that would signal the release of the lobster salad from its mold. She happened to glance at the clock on the window-sill and, noting that it was almost time for the CBC news, she left the salad hovering over its plate in the sink and walked across her kitchen to switch on her little black radio.

Once the introductory music ended, signalling the beginning of the CBC national news, she listened for new developments in the political uprising. As befitted the serious nature of what he was saying, the announcer dropped his well-modulated voice. He gave out details of the previous day's funeral for Pierre Laporte, the Minister of Labour and Immigration in the Quebec Government, whose body had been found the Sunday just past.

> *"The body of kidnap victim Pierre Laporte was borne to his last resting place yesterday. Paratroops, standing atop high buildings, guarded Prime Minister Pierre Elliott Trudeau of Canada, Premier Robert Bourassa of Quebec and a host of other dignitaries attending the funeral. The Quebec cabinet minister's strangled body was found early Sunday.*
>
> *"Paying their respects were the leaders of the federal political parties, leaders of the political parties in Quebec, federal cabinet ministers, Members of Parliament and Senators, as well as members of the Quebec National Assembly and civic leaders."*

Once this news was dispensed, the announcer's voice rose ever so slightly. He related that James Richard Cross, the second victim of the FLQ, was reported to be still alive. Then, as if the announcer had run out of new things to say, he read excerpts from the now-famous speech Prime Minister Trudeau had delivered days earlier, invoking the War Measures Act. Trudeau's reasons for invoking the Act were restated, along with a reiteration of what others had said about this unprecedented action. A tape of the late Mr. LaPorte's message to the people was replayed, stating that the War Measures Act was a vital means of stopping what he had called "a wind of madness blowing across the province."

Then, because there was still air space to be accommodated, Trudeau's taped voice filled Laura's kitchen:

> "... Society must take every means at its disposal to defend itself against the emergence of a parallel power in this country ... I think it is only, I repeat, it is only weak-kneed bleeding hearts who are afraid to take these measures..."

Laura listened to the unfolding of these terrible and tragic events in a surreal, detached way — almost as if these atrocities were happening on foreign soil, or in some remote country where the media had sprung into life overnight as a result of a war or an earthquake or some other disaster. It was as if she were far removed from the social disorder, as if the purported upcoming bloodbath was only secondary to the anger and turmoil that was still churning inside her because of last night's phone call to Kevin.

Jesse had answered Kevin's phone. This had taken Laura so much by surprise that at first she hadn't recognized Jesse's voice. She had been sure that she had been given a wrong number. "Oh, I'm sorry," she had apologized. "I asked the operator for room 1470. She must have given me the wrong room." Then, suddenly recognizing his voice, she had asked, startled, "Jesse? Is this your room? I'm sorry it's quite late. I didn't mean to wake you."

"Yes ... er ... No mistake ... Just a minute. Hold on." He had mumbled as if he had been between yawns — nonchalantly, Laura thought, as if he had half-expected, half-awaited, her intrusive call. He had immediately turned the phone over to Kevin and she had distinctly heard him say, "Kev, it's for you." It was just as if Kevin had been only a pillow away from him. His easy use of the diminutive for Kevin's name had nettled her far worse across the miles than it ever had in her physical presence. Kevin never allowed anyone to call him Kev. In the early days of their court-ship, she had called him Kev a few times, but he had quickly put a stop to it, saying that his mother had called him Kevie and it always made him feel infantile.

Kevin had been obviously flustered over Jesse answering his phone. He had immediately begun explaining that there had been a mix-up in their reservations and Jesse had had to bunk in with him. Otherwise, Kevin said, Jesse would have had to go to a hotel halfway across the city, and these were not the best of times to travel. He had explained in full, just as if he was used to being subjected to an inquisition, just as if he always had to account for his actions, just as if Jesse's inconvenience was any concern of hers.

Although Laura had gone to bed immediately after the call, she had not gone to sleep. She had been too angry with herself. First, she was angry for even having made the call; and, second, she was angry for having given Jesse the satisfaction of hearing her stumbling, think-ing she had reached a wrong number and apologizing for waking them up, when she had made the call with Kevin's safety in mind.

Certainly, Kevin hadn't appeared to be the least bit grateful for her concern. Indeed, he had sounded as if he were vexed by her anxiousness. She thought he was probably angry because he would have to explain to Jesse that she hadn't telephoned just to check up on him. She knew it would gall him no end to do that. Upon reflection, she had to admit that Kevin did have probable cause to surmise the phone call was just a ruse and her concern for his safety feigned. When she had found out he was driving to Montreal, she had suggested that she and Hannah go along. He had refused outright, saying he didn't want Hannah caught up in the FLQ mess which, from all news reports, seemed to be heating up instead of cooling down. When she had persisted, saying the drive back and forth would give them time to be together, he had said, a little too caustically she had thought, that surely she wasn't turning into one of those women who didn't trust her husband out of her sight.

Laura turned the radio off and tried to forget about Kevin and his over-explanation, and about Jesse and his proprietary air. She concentrated on the salad she had placed in the sink and which now, on account of her woolgathering had, dropped in a headlong rush out of its fancy mold, part of it landing on the plate she had placed there for that purpose and part of it clinging to the aluminum mold. Ruefully, she admitted to herself that the blob of pinkish gelatin didn't resemble any fish known to her, much less a lobster. She hoped that the Faculty Women's Arts and Crafts group would find that it tasted better than it looked. In a futile attempt to give it a little more dash, she got out the paring knife and tried to sculpt the mound of gelatin into the likeness of a probable sea creature.

When she had re-carved the gelatin to the best of her ability, she took the heaping platter to the fridge and nudged it in between yesterday's left-over spaghetti and a half-filled pickle bottle. She was careful not to disturb the plate of lemon squares and chocolate brownies that she had cautiously arranged so that one sweet didn't rub up against the other.

After the luncheon food had been prepared and stored away and the dirty dishes had been placed in the dishwasher, she surveyed her tidy kitchen with satisfaction. Everything was in readiness for the Arts and Crafts group. She smiled a tiny gratified smile as she looked at the uncluttered counters, the waxed-within-an-inch-of-its-life tile floor, the dusted off china piled neatly on the table, and the fingerprint-free fridge. She thought with satisfaction that even if the women were to surprise her and arrive a few minutes early, she was so prepared that they wouldn't be able to raise even the tiniest fluster within her.

Three women from the Arts and Crafts group — Del Whitcomb, Margaret Thompson and Judy Hardly — arrived sharply at noon and Laura ushered them into her living room. Each one clutched a basket filled with the makings of a macramé plant hanger — wooden beads, hemp, coloured string. Macramé was the "in vogue" craft of the month. The women were no sooner settled than Del asked if she could have the television turned on.

"Switch on the TV, Laura. They're going to have a replay of LaPorte's funeral," she said, dumping a yogurt carton of beads into her lap. "We can work and watch and eat at the same time." Del's shoulders twitched as she spoke, as if she were anticipating a delicious experience.

Laura crossed the floor to the television set. Within moments, the Prime Minister's voice flooded the room. Excerpts from the War Measures Speech were once more replayed.

"Doesn't he just send shivers up your spine," Del said, pausing to extract just the right size bead from her lap before shivering in an exaggerated manner. "He's so masterful. I loved it when he first began talking about the War Measures Act, especially when he said it was going to permit the full weight of Government to be brought to bear on all those persons advocating or practicing violence, and how he called those upstarts a band of cowards and murderers. He minces no words. Calls things as he sees them. And I adored him when he talked about the weak-kneed bleeding hearts." She pursed her mouth and arched her neck to give endorsement to her statement. Then she surveyed the room, asking no one in particular, "Don't you think he has just the right word for every occasion?" She giggled saucily. "He could put his boots under my bed any night."

Judy was one of the weak-kneed bleeding hearts Trudeau had castigated. Del's overblown praise of the Prime Minister was deliberately aimed directly at her, as Judy well knew. And, as Del expected, Judy picked up the gauntlet.

"The Government has no right interfering with our civil liberties. Setting curfews. Searching us for weapons. If we allow this to happen, we'll end up with a dictatorship."

Everyone in the room was aware that Judy was speaking the gospel according to John, her professor of history husband, who specialized in Conflict Studies, but even Del had the good grace not to pick her up on this.

Judy had more to say and she felt this was the time to say it. She pulled herself upright in her chair and righted the basket on her lap, as if readying herself for battle. She stretched her chin in a lofty manner, implying that anyone with a grain of liberalism would rebel against a police state being set up in the name of democracy. She posed a hypothetical situation. "Del, how would you like to be in Quebec right now and you're walking down the street and the next thing you know you're rounded up and shoved into jail and you're going to be detained for three weeks or so before you even get charged?"

Not for an instant did Del break stride from stringing together a rosary of brown beads — beads that would eventually stream from her macramé plant hanger like crystal drops from a chandelier. She pulled her mohair sweater closer around her shoulders as if it were a coat of mail.

"If that's what it takes to get rid of those damn subversives, those drugged-out terrorists, those Cuban bandits, then that's what it takes." She snapped out her words in a militant voice and quoted the patriotic phrases that had fallen on everyone's ears from every media outlet for the past several days. "Like Trudeau said, we have to root out the cancer. We have to rid ourselves of those revolutionaries who are out to destroy our country. I say, round up everyone and anyone walking on the streets. Keep them in for three months, not just three weeks, if that's what's necessary."

Laura, who was passing around napkins in preparation for bringing in the salad, paused mid-room. "Oh don't talk like that, Del," she chided, partly to deflect the conversation in a more benign direction. "Kevin is up there. Jesse is giving a paper. His first international conference. Kevin went along for moral support." She added, with a touch of pride, "Of course, Kevin co-authored the paper, but he's letting Jesse give it for the experience."

Del, whose husband was also teaching in the Social Science and Humanities Faculty, gave a dismissive hrrmph. "Oh, for the love of God, Laura, there's nothing to worry about. Not if you keep your nose clean." She then asked, strictly as a pacifying measure because she already knew the answer, "He's in the Queen Elizabeth hotel, isn't he? That's where our fellows always stay."

Laura left the women wrangling over whether downtown Montreal was in the eye of the storm, and went to the kitchen to begin preparing the lunch. Because her living room was open to the kitchen, she could hear the conversation as she moved around arranging the food.

She walked back and forth between the sink, stove and refrigerator, preparing the tea and coffee, and wondering why she continued her involvement with this group. Some of the women were very nice, but several were like Del — gossipy and small-minded. When she had a meeting with them she always came away feeling more alienated and alone than if she had been at home by herself. She chided herself for not having found a job or returned to university when they had moved back from Nova Scotia. She told herself that she should have forced Kevin to allow her to do one or the other. But he had balked at her getting a job, even though one had been offered to her in the campus library, and even though it was part-time. She could have hired a sitter for Hannah, but Kevin was worried that his colleagues would think he couldn't support his family. And when she had pushed for university, again part-time, he had said that because he was on campus, and because her father was also well-known, there would be too much pressure on her to succeed. When she had asked him, insulted, if he thought she wasn't capable of doing well — carefully pointing out that she had proved she could do well during the year she had spent in university before dropping out on account of pregnancy — he had quickly denied any such insinuation. He had straightened up in his chair and asked her, totally exasperated, "Laura, why do you twist everything I say? It is getting so I have to rehearse every sentence before I let it come out of my mouth."

Then, in a voice raw with vexation, he had spelled out what he had really meant, "I just thought you'd be more comfortable at a university where you weren't known." He had mentioned his tentative plans to spend the following summer teaching at the University of New Mexico. "I thought it would be more comfortable for you, and probably more convenient for us, if you waited until then."

She had dropped the discussion then and there, and contented herself with looking after Hannah and polishing the living-room furniture with Pledge — polishing it until she could see her reflection in the table top. And, for outside activity, she had joined the Arts and Crafts group, which met every Wednesday afternoon.

Laura removed the reconstructed seafood platter from the refrigerator and headed across the kitchen to get a handful of paper towelling to sop up the liquid that had seeped out of the gelatin onto the platter. As she did so, she heard Del, who was sorting her beads in descending order of size, say, "If I were Laura, I'd worry more about Kevin getting picked up by Jesse Morris than by the Quebec police. According to everything I've heard Jesse has leanings that way. Everyone in the Department knows that."

Laura turned at that moment and looked in through the open Dutch doors into the living room, and she was just in time to see Del gesture grandly, her wrist limp and a devilish smile on her face. "Besides, Kevin should think about his own reputation. If you walk like a duck ... Well, you know how that goes."

"Oh Del, you're outrageous," Margaret Thompson cut in. "Next thing you know you'll have poor Laura imagining Kevin and Jesse in bed together."

In that instant, searing heat, like flash lightening, surged through Laura's body, making her giddy and lightheaded. She lurched forward. The kitchen whirled around her and she had to clutch at the salad platter for support. She reeled towards the sink counter, hoping to grab hold, but she missed it by inches. Like a boat in a swell, the floor pitched upwards as if to swamp her and then just as quickly dropped back down again. She felt like Alice going down the rabbit hole. *Down. Down. Down.* She landed in a crumpled heap on the perfectly waxed black and white tiles. Pink gelatin soaked into her light grey pantsuit and it looked as if her life's blood was seeping out through the fortrel material.

As she sat there dazed and lightheaded, her life with Kevin passed before her eyes. Incriminating incident after incriminating incident piled up on top of each other. She recalled Jesse's warm sleepy voice — an after-lovemaking voice — when he had answered the phone in Kevin's room; and she remembered the fuzzy soft phone call she had heard Kevin make late one night when he had thought she was asleep — a call challenged by her, but later soundly explained by him. And, forcing herself not to be squeamish, she picked through other days — days that had not been placed before her eyes. Like the day she had accidentally pulled a magazine from Kevin's briefcase when she was moving it from where he had left it, blocking the doorway. Piqued by the cover photo of two men sharing a passionate kiss, she had flipped through the pages and what she had seen horrified her. "What are you doing with such trash," she had fairly shouted at Kevin, tossing the magazine on the table beside him.

"I'll get them for that," he had said laughing a thin laugh that wasn't solid enough to cover his bluster. "Those graduate students are always up to one prank or another."

Hearing Laura crash to the floor, the four women in the living room all rushed to the kitchen. "Oh my God in heaven, Laura, what happened?" Margaret's anxious voice reached her from a distance, and when she looked around, she saw all four women standing over her, eight pairs of hands outreached in concern.

"I'm okay," she replied hastily, and even managed a flustered laugh. "These high heels. I must've slipped on the tile."

Someone relieved her of the platter while she forced herself upright, shooing the women away and saying she was perfectly capable of standing on her own, although her knees felt as if they were going to buckle underneath her.

"I'm afraid there's not much left of the salad," she apologized shakily, surveying the mess on the floor. "Whatever is left on the plate, that's it."

"Not to worry," Del said good-naturedly. "If we don't have enough, this floor is so clean we can eat right off the tiles."

After Laura had assured the women that she had neither hurt nor broken any part of herself in the fall, and had coaxed them back to the front room, she began rescuing the lunch, salvaging the lobster salad by spooning what had remained on the platter onto individual lettuce leaves.

But, even as she parcelled out the salad, her mind was only partly on what she was doing. She continued to retrace the years of her marriage, and the very act of doing so made the pit of her stomach feel as cold as the platter from which she was scooping the salad. She wished she could sink inside herself where it would be warm and safe, but her mind, now crystal clear, raced backwards, scavenging for other signs of Kevin's homosexuality that she surely must have missed along the way. And, although she could find nothing definitive to support Del's insinuation — nothing that didn't have the shadow of a doubt attached to it — she still knew!

Judy shouted out from the living room, reminding her that a rerun of LaPorte's funeral was being televised. "Hurry up and get in here, Laura. Don't worry about the food. You don't want to miss this."

"I'll be there in a minute," she called back, her voice even, although she was at that moment leaning against the sink, sucking in air to steady herself. To keep the women from coming to the kitchen to help her, she told them not to worry — whatever she missed she would catch later on, because no doubt it would be replayed again. "Go ahead and watch," she reassured them. "Don't wait for me. I'll get a chance to see the whole thing this evening."

She pulled open the cutlery drawer and hastily rummaged for the salad forks. As she did so, she heard the television announcer's lowered voice setting the scene for the funeral:

"Several thousand people squeezed ten-deep behind barricades on streets surrounding historic Place d'Armes, where stately Notre Dame is situated, its twin grey towers dedicated to Temperance and Perseverance.

"Soldiers with automatic weapons at the ready faced the crowds, while marksmen watched from strategic rooftops. Even sewers were searched for explosives and assassins.

"Waiting onlookers murmured in quiet conversation in a chill wind as lines of cars carrying political leaders paraded into the ancient square, lights flashing. The sympathy of the nation goes out to Pierre LaPorte's widow, Francoise, his wife of twenty-five years."

When Laura entered the living room carrying a tray loaded with salad plates and forks, she was just in time to hear Del exclaim, her voice tremulous, "Imagine that! Imagine having the sympathy of a nation. Almost worth having your husband die for something like that." She repeated the phrase as if its awesomeness was mind-boggling: "Sympathy of a nation!"

Laura began to parcel out the luncheon plates, and as she did so she kept hearing Del's voice saying, "Almost worth having your husband die for something like that." By the time the last plate had been passed around, Laura was fantasizing. In her fantasy, Kevin had exchanged places with Pierre La Porte. She saw herself in Saint Anne's Anglican Church, saw herself sitting up front, in the same pew where she had sat Sunday after Sunday, childhood year after childhood year, uncomfortable yet secure between Vera and Donald MacPhail. She saw herself sitting with Hannah, their arms in semi-circles around each other, mostly for Hannah's comfort. The Dean — no, not the Dean, he wasn't in a high enough position, it would have to be the President of the university — was offering the eulogy for Kevin, lauding his life of character, and mourning his untimely death at the hands of the dastardly FLQ. And she saw herself — Laura Stevenson, a woman whose marriage had ended in honour, in death and with the sympathy of a nation — sitting in the front pew, her arm around Hannah. There was no hint of the secret that was stitched into Kevin, as surely as it was stitched into Jesse, and, in some way, as surely as it was stitched into her and into Hannah. Only with great difficulty was she able to allow her mind to give this secret a name, but she was sure that it was not one that could ever pass her lips. She felt only envy for Mrs. LaPorte.

"Blood! What blood?" Judy snapped, jolting Laura back to the present.

Del was insisting that the trunk of LaPorte's car had been filled with blood. "There was no blood!" Judy crowed, cracking the words as if she were cracking a whip, delighted to be able to give Del her comeuppance. "Not a drop. He was choked to death, for God's sake. With a religious chain he had around his neck. He wasn't shot." She reached up to her own neck and gave a satisfied tug at her gold chain. "A chain like this! Where are you getting that blood stuff from?"

Del stood corrected, but not graciously. She justified herself, "I heard it on the news that he was shot. This is the first I've heard about him being choked." Piqued at being dressed down in front of the others, she quickly let Judy know what she, a non-bleeding heart, would do if she were in charge of negotiations with the perpetrators.

"If it were left up to me, I'd send that Jacques Lanclot on the toe of my boot to Algiers if that's where he wants to go so badly. But no way would the taxpayers foot the bill."

As Del spoke, she threaded the beads on the hemp plant hanger as if she were pulling them through Lanclot's heart. "There's no way in God's green earth that our taxpayers should be paying his way. Throw him in jail in this country. Like any bloody kidnapper. And his brother Francois along with him. And that lawyer, what's his name, Lemieux, dump him in too. Like Levesque called them, they're a bunch of sewer rats."

Laura passed the last fork to Del. She wished all of them would go home. And again she wished she could trade places with Mrs. LaPorte.

During the next couple of days, while Laura waited for Kevin to return from Montreal, she walked around as if she was caught in a surreal environment, as if she was trying to wake up from a terrible nightmare. Nothing seemed centered or grounded or ordered or real. She seldom slept. She rarely ate. She felt cheated, revolted, defiled. And she felt alone. She had no one to turn to. There was no one to whom she could entrust such a terrible secret.

Then she remembered that, in times of trouble, her mother — who always kept her own counsel — had often sought comfort from the Scriptures. She found the family Bible and opened it at random. One sentence leaped out at her and obscured all the rest: "By the rivers of Babylon, there we sat down and wept." Laura, who had been unable to shed a tear since she had overheard Del's remark, sat down at her kitchen table and wept. And she wept. And wept. She cradled her face in her hands and let scalding hot tears slip out between her fingers. She felt their moist heat as they rushed down her hands and across her bare arms. Later, when she looked in the mirror, she saw their river-like tracks on her still-tanned flesh.

She wept for the young woman who had taken the English 1010 course on the British poets and who had fallen in love with Keat's *Ode to a Grecian Urn*. She recalled how she had revelled in the angst of the two lovers on the urn, eternally separated, eternally reaching, knowing they would never feel the touch of each other's flesh but always savouring the exquisite pain of hope. Her thoughts had soared deliciously above the classroom the day they had studied the poem, and she had imagined the rapturous ecstasy of having a man yearn to ravish her body as that Greek man must have yearned to ravish the body of that Greek maiden.

She wept for the young woman who, only a few years into marriage, had stepped out of her shower one day and stood naked in front of her full-length bathroom mirror. She had wiped the steam from the mirror with the tail of her towel and then, in full view of herself, had run her damp hands up and down her thighs, sliding her long slender fingers sensuously over the soft smooth skin of her belly, over the shiny, but barely visible, pregnancy stretch marks that looked like tiny pale worms making their way to her pubic hair. And, as her hands had roamed her body, she had fantasized that some man was lusting for her, a man who truly wanted her body, a man who truly ached for her flesh, a man who truly craved her womanhood. Even as she had tumbled these thoughts around, she had kept pushing guilt aside, believing she was being an emotional adulteress by entertaining those thoughts. But her guilt hadn't stopped her from continuing to luxuriate in them, imagining herself completely enveloped in some man's abandoned sexual hunger, imagining her womanhood completely affirmed by a lover's unbridled carnal appetite.

After she had had her fill of fantasizing, she had stepped back from the mirror and begun towelling herself dry. In doing so, she had accidentally knocked over a giant-sized bottle of bubble bath that was perched on the ledge of the tub. As she had picked it up to put it back in its place, she had convinced herself that the root of the trouble with her marriage bed lay in her lack of attention to erotic detail. This lack, she had thought, was epitomized in the bottle of bubble bath — a bottle she had bought for her year-old daughter, but which she, too, used because she was too frugal to buy her own brand. The garish yellow bottle was shaped like a pig. It had a spout where a navel would ordinarily be, and from this spout leaked a thick, greenish liquid. She had asked herself what kind of man could be aroused by a woman who bathed in a greenish liquid that smelled like rotting pears and that was poured out of a bottle resembling an incontinent pig.

The very next day, instead of buying groceries, she had purchased a sensual fragrance that promised nights of expanded boundaries. She had visited a lingerie shop and left with a negligee that crowded the margins of decency. And, that very same night, she had waited for her husband to come to bed. And she had waited. And she had waited. At about eleven o'clock, Kevin had hollered up the stairs. He had urged her to go to sleep because he had to do some polishing on a paper on deviant behaviour and it would probably take all night.

Knowing Kevin's penchant for reasoned evidence, while Laura waited for him to return from Montreal she spent her nights culling evidence, separating fact from surmise or suspicion. Each night, as she lay wide awake in bed, she used her left hand as if it were an abacus and pulled her fingers this way for fact, that way for conjecture. Mostly her fingers were pulled to the side of conjecture. For example, one incident that she placed on the side of conjecture had occurred on the summer day she had gone to the garage to tell Kevin he had a phone call. She had found him there with Jesse, and she had felt from the fluster in the air that she had surprised them. But at what? The moment only took on importance now, in the light of Del's gossip.

And she remembered the day she had walked into Kevin's study unexpectedly and found him hunched over his desk, his shoulders convulsing from great wracking sobs that echoed in the empty room. When she had anxiously asked him what was wrong, he had mumbled a dismissive, "Nothing. Nothing at all." But when he had looked at her, she had seen that his eyes blazed raw, naked pain.

She had been terrified that day — terrified of the tears, terrified of the raw pain in his face, terrified of what these emotions meant for him, meant for her, for their child, for their marriage. For one pulse-stopping second she had wanted to run from the room and pretend she had never entered it. But then she had pushed her fear aside and, awash with compassion, had gone to him and cradled his head against her breast. She had asked over and over what was wrong, but he would only say that he wasn't good enough for her and Hannah, that both of them deserved better. But when she had assured him that he was an excellent father, a good husband, he had shaken his head and sobbed, "My life's a mess. I've messed up everyone's life."

At the time she had surmised that he was upset because his research was falling behind and because his proposal for new research money had been turned down. They had clung to each other for a long time and she had repeated, "It'll get better. Everything will work out. Just give it time." His pain had been so bare that she had cried too. (In hindsight, Laura feels certain that those moments in Kevin's den, those moments when they were cradled in each other's arms, crying together, were the purest moments of their marriage. They were purer even than the birth of Hannah. And even though she now has a better notion of why Kevin was crying, they are still not moments she would be willing to forfeit.)

She spent night after night segregating the evidence of Kevin's infidelity, categorizing it into piles — this pile conjecture, that pile fact. At the end of the organizing, she could see that there was a heavy weighting on the side of conjecture. Her spirits then lifted. She decided that when Kevin got home she would warn him about the gossip that was circulating on campus about Jesse. She even considered confessing — in a light, tossing-off sort of way, of course, so Kevin would know how far off the mark she had allowed her emotions to go — that after she had heard Del's gossip she had harboured her own suspicions, not only about Jesse, but about him and Jesse. If he hotly denied Del's accusation about Jesse, and tossed off her own suspicions as being too ridiculous to comment upon (as she hoped he would do, because what would she do if he didn't?) she would then carry on as she had carried on for the last three years — accepting his excuses, his unpredictable absences, his less than cork tight alibis, his rumpled shirts, his limited sexual overtures.

The evening Kevin pulled into the driveway, exhausted, he said, from the drive home, she waited until they were in bed before she brought up the subject of Del's gossip.

As soon as Kevin kissed her good night — just a peck of a kiss — he immediately turned his back to her, mumbling as if he were already half asleep, something about having an early class in the morning.

She lay beside him, frustrated and unrumpled, as if she were still alone in the bed, her new ivory-coloured satin nightgown — the one she had bought for his homecoming, prior to Del's disclosure — undisturbed from ankle to shoulder. She stared up at the white stucco ceiling, up into the blackness of the room. A shaft of light from a street lamp angled in through the window and fell on Kevin's face. The fresh smell from the morning's line-dried sheets wafted around her. She put her arm down by her left side so that it filled up the space between her body and Kevin's. He moved ever so slightly, as if in sleep — just enough to break contact with her flesh.

She hoisted herself up on one elbow and said softly, "Kevin." He didn't answer, but she knew by the guilty flutter of his eyelids and the small twitches of his body that he was as wide awake as she was. She lay back down and spoke matter-of-factly, not changing her position on the bed, not even turning her head toward him. And she made her pronouncement.

"Del Whitcomb says Jesse Morris is a homosexual." She said the word out loud for the very first time in connection with Jesse. "She says everyone knows it." She laughed lightly, about to say that she had been absurd enough to think that perhaps there was some sexual connection between Kevin and Jesse, but she never got the chance to get these words out of her mouth. Kevin whipped around so fast that he jerked the sheet from her side of the bed, and she felt a sudden chill, even though the room was quite warm. Along with the chill, she could feel the heat from the blaze of fury coursing through his body.

"Hasn't that old gossip anything better to do than to go around tearing strips off people," Kevin rasped, seemingly no longer weary. Although she could only see the outline of his face because his head now blocked the light from the window, she knew from the tone of his voice that his nostrils were pinched and his eyes were flashing heat. "Better still," he charged, "haven't you got anything better to do than to listen to her?"

"Is he?" she persisted, ignoring his insult, her body by now perspiring, fearful of his answer. She had hoped for an immediate denial, hoped that he would laugh uproariously and give some jock response about the absurdity of anyone considering Jesse to be anything other than a male stud, a woman's man.

"How should I know?" he flared, talking to the ceiling, in the same way as she was talking to the ceiling. "I don't go around asking a person's sexual preference. Besides, what difference does it make? His business is his business." He jerked the sheets again in preparation for turning away. "Now I'm dead tired, so let's drop the subject. And I never want to hear anything like that again."

Laura was certain that the conversation was making Kevin uncomfortable, really unnerving him, because it wasn't like him to let a controversial topic go without a demand for facts. Under ordinary circumstances he pressed for particulars, and when she couldn't produce an overwhelmingly large body of evidence he considered the argument won by default.

"I can't drop the subject," she said, wishing she could. "Not until I get an answer from you. You're closer to him than anyone, I'm sure you know one way or the other. If others know, surely you know." She waited for a moment, the silence heavy, and then, in a voice bloated with fear, she asked, "I need to know, Kevin. Are you and Jesse having an affair?"

Kevin bolted upright, all signs of sleep instantly disappearing. "Are you mad?" he demanded, his voice stiff from the bite of his anger. "Have you gone totally mad?"

She sat up too. On the one hand, she was intensely relieved by his anger. It showed the extent of her madness. But, on the other hand, she knew it only showed the extent of Kevin's anger at her accusation. Like a pesky mosquito that knows it will get slapped away each time it lands, she kept at him.

"Then explain about the day …" She catalogued the several incidents she had memorized on the nights she had lain in bed unable to sleep.

Furiously, Kevin refuted each incident. Of course he and Jesse had looked embarrassed when she walked into the garage that day. Jesse had asked him for a loan and because he knew she had never liked him, he didn't want her to know about it. And hadn't he already explained about the magazine? And why he had to share the room with Jesse in Montreal?

She lay back down in the bed and began to cry, not knowing whether she was crying because she couldn't get at the truth, or whether what she had taken for the truth wasn't truth at all.

He, too, inched back down in the bed and leaned into her then, startling her by reaching out to hold her. He even brushed her tears away with the heel of his hand. "You've got to stop listening to those gossips, Laura," he said in a voice that held forgiveness. "You've got to do it for your own good." His tone hardened. "And Del should look into her own husband's character before she attacks other people's." He doled out information that was both new and shocking and that placed Del's gossip in a different perspective — one which he knew would steer them to a different subject.

"I think you should know that it was Weldon Whitcomb who shafted me out of some research money. And Del knows it, too. She can say what she likes about Jesse but he would never backstab anyone like that. Weldon is jealous of him. Jealous enough to start a rumour. And of me, too, for that matter. Thinks we're the movers and shakers. And we're going to show up the Old Guard by the amount of research we can turn out."

He added, his tone softening again, "I promise you I'll keep my distance from Jesse as much as possible. But he is my graduate student. And although I know you've never liked him, I'm going to have to be associated with him for the next six or eight months, until he gets his dissertation done. Maybe even after that. Dalhousie wants him back, and we're in the same field. I'm bound to run across him at conferences."

Her anxieties deflated by Kevin's stormy denial, by his inflamed negations and by his unexpected caress, Laura allowed the conversation to veer away from Jesse and towards Weldon Whitcomb. Afterwards, she put her head on Kevin's chest and circled her free arm around his shoulders. She felt him draw a deep breath and then let it out — in resignation or relief, she wasn't sure. But at least he didn't turn away from her.

Although Jesse never came to the house again, he was as immutably with Kevin and Laura as if he lay between them in the marital bed. He crowded the sheets. He hogged the pillows. Laura could smell him on the mattress. She could hear his swaggering, little cough-type laugh whenever her and Kevin's attempts at lovemaking fizzled into disappointment. She could see him standing beside her whenever Kevin returned from a trip and she searched his suitcase for signs of unfaithfulness: musky shirts, rakish undershorts that weren't worn at home and which Kevin explained by pretending to have forgotten to pack his Fruit of the Loom cottons.

And she could see Jesse in Kevin's quick, jaunty stride as he left the house each morning — a stride that also wasn't worn at home. She could see him in Kevin's credit card receipts. She could smell him in the stale leavings of Mennen aftershave — Jesse's signature scent. But in her need to keep her marriage intact, Laura steadfastly negated and blindly overlooked all of these signs whenever she came upon them. For her own sake and for Hannah's sake, and with enough denials from Kevin, she was able to persuade herself that Jesse Morris had no special place in Kevin's life.

E i g h t

Hannah slows the car to a crawl because she has come upon construction work on the Quebec highway. She looks at Laura, who is leaning back against the seat, her eyes closed.

"Yo! Wake up," she says. "We're well into Quebec. Are you going to sleep the whole trip?" Hannah yawns and stretches exaggeratedly. "It's so boring, this drive." She looks at Laura and says pointedly, "Unless, of course, you can sleep the whole time."

Laura denies being asleep. "I was just resting my eyes and listening to your music." She hums a few bars from *Born Free*, "Born Free. As free as the wind …" She breaks off. "I didn't know you had such eclectic tastes in music.

"Is that good or bad?" Hannah asks suspiciously. "I'm no English major, you know."

Laura laughs. "It's good. It's just that I never realized you liked such a wide variety of music. I thought you'd be into nothing but rap or whatever is the latest thing on the go. It just surprises me that I didn't know your taste in music."

"Oh there's plenty about me you don't know," Hannah replies quickly, but not caustically. Then, giving her words a definite weight, she adds, "And I'm beginning to realize there's plenty about you I don't know."

Laura sits up straight and reaches over and turns the volume down on the tape deck. She says, surprising Hannah, "I think it's really sad that we think we know people, know all about them. Just

124

because we love them we think we know them. But we don't know them at all. I'm coming to realize that there are dimensions to all of us that even those closest to us never realize are there."

She relates to Hannah a story a teacher had told in the faculty lounge one noon hour just a few days earlier. The teacher's mother had died and the teacher had gone back to Ontario for the funeral. Her younger sister had wanted to place something special in her mother's casket — something her mother had enjoyed during her lifetime. After thinking about it a bit, this sister had hit upon the idea of buying some special candies that she knew had been her mother's favourites. She had announced that she was going to buy several boxes of M&Ms and sort out the dark brown ones, because these were the ones her mother had liked best. The teacher then had to inform her younger sister that her mother had hated the dark brown M&Ms; she had eaten them only because the rest of the family left them uneaten.

Laura's musings trigger Hannah to pick up the conversation they had dropped earlier. She does this as if only a few seconds have passed since she first asked Laura about her reasons for threatening to leave her father last spring.

"So what was all that about? Why were you going to leave Dad?" Hannah squirms around in the seat and squares her shoulders, as if she is bracing herself to hear something unpleasant.

Laura remains noncommittal. "I had my reasons. I told you he lied to me about something. It was important to me but not to you, so I'm not going to discuss it any further. I already told you that." She then says, in a manner reminiscent of her own mother whenever the young Laura had asked questions to which she wasn't entitled to have answers, "Like your grandmother used to say to me whenever I nosed into areas that weren't my concern, 'Children, even only children, shouldn't be given total access to their parents' marriage. There are things inside every marriage that should be kept between the two partners.'"

Hannah pulls her mouth taut but says nothing. Because Laura is afraid that Hannah will revert to her chilly silence of the morning, and because she needs to set her straight about her jealousy of Kevin, she says gently, "You're wrong about me being jealous of everyone your father talked to on the phone. Or of everyone he talked to anywhere, for that matter. I certainly wasn't." She then decides that she wants to be relentlessly honest. "A slight revision on what I just said. I had my select jealousies. I was jealous of you. Like you said awhile ago. You had such easy access to your father's affections. It really tormented me that I had to pick and choose times when I could show him affection, but you could be so free-wheeling about it. And you took it so much for granted. You were so cavalier about it." She quickly adds, "But I'm not holding that against you. Every child has a right to take parental love for granted. I guess what I'm getting at is that it hurt me when you used to push me to the sidelines. And I was so needy for love."

Laura shoots Hannah a fast, sideways glance and readies herself for an impatient retort about the conversation becoming too maudlin. Instead, however, Hannah simply explains why she had hoarded her affection for her mother and yet gave it so willingly to her father."I always felt you didn't like me. I felt you resented me. That's why I favoured Dad. I never doubted he loved me."

She twists her shoulders and opens and closes her fingers on the wheel, as if she is revving up her nerve to make a clean breast of things. "But I must confess, I was a bit devious. I knew it got to you. About Dad and me, I mean. I sometimes deliberately baited you. Especially if you had been mean to me over something. Didn't let me stay out as late as I wanted to, or whatever."

She explains further. "I thought you spoiled things for us. Just for meanness, I used to think. I remember I'd be sitting on Dad's lap and he'd say, 'Let's go, young lady, and get some ice cream for you,' and you'd say, real short like, 'She's had enough sweets for today.' Or sometimes you'd say, 'You're going to rot her teeth,' or some downer like that, and spoil everything. Dad would never argue with you, but in a few minutes he'd put me down, saying he had work to do. I'd be so mad at you then."

"I'm sorry," Laura says, contritely, thinking of the wasted years. "I'm really sorry. For whatever reason, we seemed to have shortchanged each other."

Not knowing whether this is the appropriate time or not for such revelations, she now decides to tell Hannah that she has always felt unnecessary, so non-central to everyone's life.

She says, "Maybe you don't want to hear this, but I always felt so unessential. It was as though everyone had someone except me. Mother and Father had each other. You had your Dad. And your Dad had you." She almost says "and your Dad had Jesse," but stops short of doing so.

She tells Hannah about Mary/Joseph, about how she imagined him being a little boy with dark blond hair like hers, only in summer it would become more gold-streaked than hers. And she relates how she was sure Mary/Joseph would have known when she needed a hug, or a kiss, or even just a smile. And she tells Hannah that she thinks, if Mary/Joseph had lived, he would have been *her* someone — and then, perhaps, she wouldn't have been so stingy in her dealings with Hannah.

Her eyes water as she says this, and she blinks back stinging tears, hoping Hannah will permit her one or two more sentences before making a gagging sound, signalling that her mother is pushing the margins of sickening sentimentality.

"I had such hopes for us, so many mother and daughter dreams. Gram and I were never really close. I think it was because she was already middle-aged when I was born. And because she doted on Granpy. And Granpy was all caught up in his work. They loved me. But they didn't really need me. When you were born, I thought things would be different. Because I really needed you. I was convinced that my whole life would be totally interwoven with yours, and instead ..."

She lets her words trail off, and shamefacedly remembers how she had selfishly tried to keep Hannah from going to kindergarten because she would have been so lonely in the house without her. And she remembers how, when Kevin had insisted on the child going to school, she had used this incident as a showdown with him to get her own way.

The incident had happened when Hannah was four — approximately three years after Jesse had been made *persona non grata* in the Stevenson household. It was a Monday morning. She had stepped out of the shower stall and once more confronted her naked self in the full-length mirror on the bathroom door. She had seen a young woman with slim hips, small waist and narrow shoulders. And she had seen a woman with shiny, sun-streaked, shoulder-length brown hair. And she had also seen a woman with grieving eyes, a wounded smile, and hands that fidgeted as if they were constantly looking for things to do to fill the spaces in her life.

Just a few hours later that very same day, Kevin had come home for lunch and excitedly told her that there was going to be a kindergarten set up on the university campus. "Faculty children are going to be given first choice," he had said, his voice exuberant. "The best of teachers. Quite experimental. On the cutting edge of pedagogy. Tremendous opportunity for Hannah." He had looked at Hannah, who was at the end of the table mashing an Oreo cookie into her milk. "I signed her up for the mornings in September."

"You've done what?" Laura had said, horrified, seeing her days stretching ahead of her even longer and emptier than they were now. "You've done what?"

He had repeated, "I entered Hannah in kindergarten. The spaces were filling up so I had to do it right away. I called you but you must've been out in the yard or in the shower."

She had protested vehemently, overwhelmed by the impact this would have on her life. "You shouldn't have signed her up without checking with me. I don't want her in school yet."

Kevin had looked baffled. He was beginning to understand her less and less. Other wives would have been ecstatic at such news. He had even mentioned that the Dean's wife belonged to a quilting bee that met every Tuesday morning, and suggested that, with Hannah in kindergarten, Laura would have the free time to join this group.

Hannah had squealed with delight when Kevin had asked her if she would like to go to school in the mornings just like the rest of the kids on the street, and this had prevented Laura from trying to veto his decision. She had simply watched despairingly as

Hannah jumped down from her chair and rushed over and put her arms around her father. She had known right then that all of her frantic opposition would be to no avail.

"Oh goodie, goodie. I'm going to school. Oh, thank you, Daddy," Hannah had squealed.

Later, after an exuberant Hannah had gone out to tell the neighbours that she was going to school in the fall, Kevin had found Laura sitting on the edge of their queen-size bed, crying.

"What's with you, Laura?" he had asked, exasperated. "What is so wrong with Hannah going to kindergarten? It'll be good for the child. She needs structured play."

Laura had wiped her eyes with a pot holder she had carried away from the table, and absently fiddled with the crocheted bedspread — it was one she had made the first winter she was back in Fredericton, and it had won honourable mention at the Fredericton Exhibition of Handicrafts. She had made it just to prove that she could "do" crafts if her mind was set that way, which it wasn't. She wished she could tell Kevin that she was fed up with making ceramic doodads and participating in other make-work programs, and that the last group she wanted to be part of was a quilting bee. Instead, she had bluntly asked, "How come there's money for Hannah to go to school, but there's never any for me to take a course at university?"

Taken completely off guard, Kevin had pulled a handkerchief from his pocket and wiped his forehead. In his fluster, he must have forgotten his past reasons for quashing her desire to go to university, because he now offered new ones. "It will take up too much of your time and Hannah needs you to be at home when she gets back from kindergarten." His hand had then swept the room to show the amount of neediness that awaited her right there in her house, and he had added, "It's one thing to take one of those non-credit courses and a whole other thing to take a degree course." Then he repeated his concern of two years earlier — that she might bite off more than she could chew.

"I wouldn't mind the work. I'd welcome the challenge," she had answered, and reminded him that he had promised she could go to university in New Mexico, but had reneged on that as well.

"We couldn't get a sitter we could trust," he had said, hotly defending himself. Again, his hand had swept the room, so that this time it took in the whole house and her whole life. It took in the highly polished mahogany furniture, the clean-as-a-whistle soft-toned oriental rug, the new olive green appliances in the kitchen, even the piano they had bought at a bargain price on the off chance that Hannah might want to take lessons. "In the name of God," he had asked, totally perplexed, "why aren't you ever satisfied?"

Laura had risen from the bed then. It was as if she had not heard Kevin nor seen his outswept hand. She had spoken as if she were making a plea for her life. "If Hannah goes to kindergarten," she had said confidently, knowing full well that Kevin wouldn't hold out on Hannah after telling her she could go, "I'm going back to university. I'll start in the fall. I'm not going to be put off any longer."

Anticipating another lesson in budgets and the cost of living, she had short-circuited this argument by saying that she was going to ask her mother for the tuition. "They put the money away for my education years ago," she had explained. "And they've never touched it. I know that. I've heard them say that often enough. I'll convince them to let me have it now. I'd rather have it now than after they're dead. I won't want it then. And I'll make them see that I can work around Hannah's schedule."

After making this demand, Laura had wondered why she had cowered for so long at the thought of broaching the subject. Surprisingly, Kevin had capitulated without further argument. However, as part of his acquiescence, and not unexpectedly, she had had to make a compromise — a face-saving compromise, she surmised. He would consent to her taking credit courses only if she entered an education program.

"If you insist on taking degree courses," he had told her, as if there was no way he could keep her from her folly, "then you're going to take something worthwhile, like education courses — something practical that will offer you a job later on. Give you a profession." He had elaborated. "If you head into Arts, in three years you'll be right back where you started, complaining you have nothing to do. At least if you become a teacher you can be home when Hannah is home. And your day is done at three o'clock."

Returning from her reverie, Laura glances at Hannah, who is humming softly to herself, apparently undisturbed by Laura's long pause. Laura resumes her musing, ruefully reflecting on Kevin's assumptions about a teacher's working hours, and how misguided these had been. She recalls a recent conversation to that effect.

When Laura had graduated with her teaching degree, there had been a job waiting for her in a junior high school on the outskirts of Fredericton. Her friend Lottie, who had been teaching at the same school for many years, had put in a good word for her, and this had gone a long way towards her getting the job. Of course, the fact that she had graduated with honours and at the top of her class were also factors.

Because Lottie lived on the same street as Laura, they decided to carpool and, to this day, ten years later, they still use the same transportation system — one week Laura drives her car, the next week Lottie takes hers. Over the years, they have established a social pattern, although not in any conscious way. On the drive to the school they always sit in unaffronted silence, knowing they won't have one moment of silence for the next seven or eight hours. On the return trip, however, their chatter runs non-stop. They hold postmortems on the day's happenings, and discuss whatever else is of concern to them. For Laura, the "whatever else" is usually Kevin and Hannah. For Lottie, it is her husband, Jerome.

Jerome is a research scientist with the provincial government — an entomologist, specializing in the spruce budworm. He knows all there is to know about everything that creeps and crawls in the forest, about insect eggs and larvae and tree defoliation, but he knows very little about Lottie. Indeed, Lottie often jokes, in a slightly sardonic way, that she would get more attention from Jerome if she were a woolly aphid or a balsam looper or some other creepie crawlie that Jerome could spear on a pin and look at through a microscope.

Lottie and Laura know the ins and outs of each other's lives — at least, the surface ins and outs. Laura once asked Lottie why she and Jerome stayed together if the marriage was so unsatisfying and Lottie, in her roguish way, said that it was on account of the children. Since Lottie and Jerome don't have any children, this was as good an answer as any to a question for which Laura, herself, had no better answers.

Lottie is an attractive woman. She isn't tall, but she walks with a long, haughty stride that makes her appear tall and leggy. She wears her jet black hair pulled back in a classy chignon, and her manner of dressing often borders on the delightfully outrageous. Despite her striking appearance, though, she swears that if she ever went missing Jerome would be hard pressed to describe her to the police.

Indeed, once, as a way of proving this point, she rented a room in the Beaverbrook Hotel and spent the night there without telling Jerome, hoping her unexplained absence would serve as a wake-up call for him. But, as bad luck would have it, that was the weekend the heating system failed in Jerome's laboratory and he had to spend every moment with flashlights and candles to keep his larvae from freezing. He called home to let her know what was happening, but, of course, he didn't get any answer so he left a message on the answering machine. Lottie only got his message after she returned home the next morning. To this very day, Jerome is none the wiser about her stay at the hotel.

On the Friday evening prior to this year's Thanksgiving weekend — the weekend of Laura and Kevin's revelation to Hannah — both Laura and Lottie had arrived at the same time at the back of the school parking lot, where they always park their car. It was Lottie's turn to drive, and she had unlocked the doors and then thrown an armful of examination booklets onto the back seat. "Teaching is a jest of God on all those who think it is a nine-to-five job," she had grumbled, tossing the books helter-skelter. "I'll be lucky if I even have time enough to take a bath over the weekend."

"Right on," Laura had acknowledged, adding that it had certainly been a jest of God on Kevin. She explained Kevin's notion of public school teaching — at least the notion he had had before she had become a teacher — by relating how Kevin had said to her that she should take education courses so she could get a plush teaching job in the public schools and have all sorts of free time for Hannah. She gave a wry laugh as she placed her briefcase on the floor and dropped one armload of assignments on top of Lottie's pile, keeping a second armload to lay on her lap. "Some free time! And I have to drive Hannah back to Laval on Tuesday. I don't know how I'm ever going to get this stuff corrected."

Lottie had settled herself in the driver's seat, lit up a cigarette and shooed the smoke out the open window. She had then turned to Laura, who was still trying to arrange books and purse and test papers on her lap and said, "Well, by the look of things, you'll at least get a break from this stuff come January. Congratulations, girl! Old Stangie really made the most of it over the PA system." She mimicked the principal: "'One of our teachers, Mrs. Laura Stevenson, has done us proud by obtaining a grant from the Department of Education to go down in the States in January to study all about reading problems.'" She took another long draw on her cigarette and waved the smoke away from her face, grimacing as if the smoke were distasteful. "I clapped for you when the announcement came on. In fact, my whole class clapped."

"Thanks, friend," Laura had replied. "But I nearly died when Stangroom made such a public issue of it. He sure loves that PA system. He loves the drama of interrupting a class."

Laughing, Lottie had agreed. "Yeah. I think it gives him a rush knowing the whole class is holding its breath waiting for what will come next. The way he breaks in 'Attention all classes! Attention all classes!' The drama of it all. Everyone expects he's going to announce that New Brunswick has been invaded by Martians or that they caught members of the IRA slinking in the corridors with armloads of bombs, or something equally epochal.

And then he says something like 'A notebook has been found in the girls' lavatory.' I always hear this big swoosh of collective disappointment from my class, as much as to say, 'Oh God, the school is not going to blow up after all. She's still going to be able to teach Maritime Studies.'"

This said, Lottie had changed the subject abruptly, a habit of hers that Laura has had to adjust to. "That was quick. Getting the grant, I mean. And the sabbatical leave. It usually takes a year. And you didn't put in for it until May."

Laura had nodded her agreement. "Yes, indeed. I think they hurried it up because there's such a need in our district. I heard that two other teachers also got grants for the same area of study."

Lottie had doused her cigarette in the ashtray and again abruptly changed the subject.

"Two questions, Laura," she had said. "Not that I should know or anything, but what's Kevin going to say about you leaving him for six months, and what's Hannah going to say about you leaving her precious daddy to fend for himself?"

"Well, Kevin is all right with it," Laura had said, neglecting to say that she no longer cared what Kevin said about her going. "He knows I can't get the courses here."

She had hated telling Lottie half-truths, but she couldn't very well have said that the reason she had applied for the grant and the sabbatical leave in the first place was to get away from Kevin, and also that it was a way to ease into a divorce that was to take place sometime down the road. And she couldn't have told Lottie that Kevin had even suggested the sabbatical leave as a stop-gap approach.

"Yeah, he's really all right with it?" Lottie had asked sceptically, pursing her lips to blow strands of hair from her forehead — a mannerism of hers that she employs when she doesn't believe what is being said but doesn't intend to press for the truth. "Does that go for Hannah, too? She doesn't mind either?"

Laura had shaken her head. "I'm not sure. We haven't told her yet. Kevin says we should do it when she comes home for Thanksgiving. I'm for waiting until Christmas. But he says the earlier the better. Says we've got to remember she's a student."

"Oh, speaking of students," Lottie had then cut in, changing the subject once more. "I heard that Sloan was back in school today. Did he go to your class?"

Laura had burst out laughing, partly from relief that they had veered from the subject of Kevin, and partly because of the incident that had occurred in her classroom.

"Was he ever in my class! You've got to hear this." She took her hands from the assignments on her lap and placed them momentarily over her face, as if she wanted to block out the memory of Sloan. "Oh, he was there, all right. No mistaking that." She rolled her eyes upward. "I swear to God that one of these days he's going to drive me violently mad. I'm going to end up like that geography teacher a couple of years back, Amos something or other. Stripping naked in the corridor and getting carted off to the burnt-out farm."

"Oh God, yes. Poor Amos. Remember him? Amos Pendergast, that was his name," Lottie had confirmed and then, in a hilariously comical way, she had pretended she was ripping off her clothes. "I can see you now, racing up the corridor, tearing off your blouse as you go, and shouting 'What is the longest mountain range in Canada?'"

Laughing, Laura had corrected her. "Only, I'll be shouting, 'Sound out the word, Sloan. Sound out the word. Does it have a long or short vowel?'" She shook her head in amazement. "You'll never guess what he did today! I thought I was going to lose it with him for sure. We were doing long and short vowels and he was sitting there — you know how he sits — as bored as if he'd rather be cleaning out sewers. Well, in the middle of the class, he puts up his hand and says he knows some short vowels and why don't I ask him to name some."

Laura had interrupted her story to rearrange books on her lap that were beginning to slide onto the floor. She had quickly huddled them back together on her knees. Then she had shaken her head, but this time in self-chastisement. "Now, I should have known better. But here I am, my ego all fluffed up because he's responding in my class when he would only clam up in other classes. I'm already picturing a movie about me. *To Ma'am with Love*. Or *Blackboard Jungle*. So off he struts to the chalkboard and writes 'fu-k' and 'sh-t.'"

Lottie's laughter had filled the car. In fact, she had laughed so hard that her smoker's cough had taken over, and between coughs she had rasped, "Oh my God! Oh my God! How did you handle that one?"

"Like you said back there, it was as if they all drew in their breath on cue." Laura had made a swooshing sound and then swooped her hand in the air as if she were pushing the air from the car. "It was like a great swooshing surge of breath. I could almost feel it sucking me off my feet. The only thing I could think of doing was to do nothing at all, so I pretended he hadn't done anything outlandish. I turned to the class and said, 'Is Sloan right? Are the "u" and the "i" both short?' They shouted back a collective 'Yeees' and I just said, 'Thanks, Sloan,' and moved on with the lesson."

With her right hand Lottie had begun fumbling in her purse for a tissue to wipe the laugh tears from her eyes. After she had found one and was hurriedly dabbing at her eyes, she had prophesied ominously, "Well, it's a long time till December. I hope you're up to it. There'll be a lot more 'fu-ks' and 'sh-ts' now that he's found his mouth."

After that conversation, they had driven along in silence until they had come to a stop sign. Then Lottie had looked across the seat at Laura and let her eyes roam over her, sizing her up and down. After a few seconds, she had commented, a roguish little twist to her mouth, "You know, Laura, I haven't seen you look this good in years. I meant to say that to you yesterday. You've got that glow. Early pregnancy or early lust. Either will do it." She had rummaged in her purse again, this time for another cigarette, and had pulled out a half-empty pack and pushed the cigarette lighter into position. While she had waited for the lighter to pop back out, she had said, half-joking, half-earnest, "If I didn't know you as well as I do, I'd say you had a lover stashed away all summer at Macquapit Lake. I swear to God, when you came back from there you were positively radiant."

Lottie had lit the cigarette and taken a long satisfying drag on it. Then, with a saucy toss of her head, she had said, "On the other hand, maybe there's no one stashed away at the lake. Maybe academics aren't as sexually impoverished as I've been led to think." She had reflected for a second. "Of course, it could be the separation. You were at the cottage for almost three months last summer. And Kevin was off, like the young people say, doing his own thing." She had relaxed her body against the back of the seat and made as if she were pushing the wheel away from her — as if she were thinking deeply. She had then said, the wicked grin back on her face, "If I thought that's all it took — a few months' separation — I'd encourage Jerome to go on a spruce budworm expedition to the North Pole. It would have to be at least that far away. I don't think a few months at Macquapit Lake would be of any use to us. In fact, if I thought I could get the glow you have, I'd tell him to spend the next ten years up there."

Now as Laura recalls her fun times with Lottie, she asks herself why she has been more successful with friendships than with motherhood.

She rearranges the question and then discomposes Hannah by putting it to her: "Would you believe I have very loyal friends?"

"What kind of a stupid question is that?" Hannah asks tightly, wary of where the conversation might be leading.

"I was just thinking that I have really good friends. Just a handful, mind you."

"Like Smokestack Lottie," Hannah replies, her tone still a little short.

"And Frances, down in Halifax. I met her the first year I was married and we've never lost touch with each other. And Janet, my friend all through public school. And Barbara. I met her when I was at university."

"So!" Hannah says, suspiciously. "Is this a trick question or something? Why shouldn't I believe you can hold on to a few friends?"

A possible reason for the question suddenly dawns on Hannah. She says, noncommittally, "Are you wondering whether you'll see the back of their heads when they find out about your little escapade at the lake?

"In a way, yes," Laura admits. "If I tell them, I'm wondering if they'll think less of me. And if I don't tell them, I'll feel I'm being deceitful."

Hannah gives a small ironic laugh. "You mean you're worried over being deceitful about your deceitfulness."

Because there is nothing Laura can say to either add to or take away from what Hannah has just said, she lets the words hover between them. For a split second, she is tempted to tell Hannah all about Claude, all about Claude's wife, all about Jesse and all about Kevin. She is sick of her fist-clenched secrets, sick of her solitary grief. She is tempted to tell Hannah why she went to the lake by herself this past summer and why Kevin found things to do that made it look natural for him not to join her.

N i n e

Laura's decision to move to the lake was made in May, just after Kevin returned home from being away at the Learneds Conference. He had moaned and groaned about going to the conference, saying it would take too much time away from his departmental work. When she had suggested that he stay home, however, he had said that it was imperative that he go because, months earlier, when he had had more time, he had committed himself to chairing a meeting at one of the sessions.

As was her custom, she went to the airport to meet his plane when he returned, and on the drive back she reminded him that they had to go to the Dean's barbecue that evening. It was the annual spring break cook-out for faculty and graduate students before everyone scattered for the summer.

Although they were running late, Kevin insisted on taking a shower, saying as he headed for the bathroom that it had been a long, hard day for him and he wanted to refresh himself before facing the Dean's over-cooked steaks and under-cooked potatoes.

He was no sooner in the shower, the water running full tilt, than she remembered that the gas gauge on the car had been registering on empty. To save time and to save Kevin trouble, she decided to get a fill-up while he was getting ready. She went to the bathroom and asked him for his Shell credit card.

"In my wallet," he answered, his voice muffled by the running water. "On the bureau."

She went to the bedroom and picked up the dark brown leather wallet from where it lay surrounded by a couple of soiled handkerchiefs, a bunch of keys and the recently-used airline boarding pass. She flipped the wallet open and pulled out the plastic container that held all of their credit cards. She hurriedly flipped through them, searching for the gold-coloured card. It was nowhere to be found! But she did find other gas cards — none of them familiar and all of them from companies she hadn't been aware they had ever dealt with. Perplexed, she took a closer look at the contents of the wallet and then she saw what she had failed to see earlier — that Jesse Morris' name was on all of the cards. It was not just on the gas cards — it was on a Mastercharge card, a video rental card, a bank instant teller card, and on a card from a car rental agency. Still not understanding, she began rummaging through every compartment. Jesse's identification was on every item she came across — driver's licence, social insurance card, medical insurance card.

As she stood on the small, oval oriental rug beside her bed, holding the wallet and trying to make sense out of something that made no sense at all, comprehension dawned. Not all at once, but in a piecemeal sort of way. First one truth and then another and another. This wasn't Kevin's wallet. It was Jesse's! Because it was identical in colour and kind to Kevin's, Kevin must have picked it up by mistake. But under what circumstances?

With a cunning developed from years of mistrust, she began probing her mind to discover how this mistake could have occurred. And suddenly the answer exploded in her brain: Both wallets had been laid side by side on the bureau in Kevin and Jesse's shared hotel room! The explosion was so loud that she was sure she had opened her mouth and let it out in a banshee type of wail, and she had to quickly cock her ear towards the bathroom to see if the water was still running to insure that Kevin hadn't heard.

Just moments after unearthing this knowledge, the full implication of it dawned on her, and the strength drained from her legs. She stumbled towards the bed and lowered herself down on the edge of it: Kevin and Jesse were having an affair. Even more shocking, they had been having an affair during all of her married life, beginning in Halifax.

A sharp pain shot through her body, originating somewhere in the pit of her heart. She drew in her breath and it ended on a little catch-like cough, reminiscent of Jesse. Del's words from years past rushed in to confirm any doubts she might still be entertaining: "If you walk like a duck and quack like a duck and associate with ducks, it must be assumed that you are a duck." Of course, Del hadn't recited the complete saying, but she had said enough — enough for any wife who had been interested in learning the truth, or enough for any wife who had the strength to learn the truth.

As she sat on the bed, Laura could feel the heat rising from her neck to her face — flaming heat. Had people known back then? Had they pitied her all these years? Or did they know? Had Kevin and Jesse managed to keep it as secret from others as they had from her?

She held the open wallet in her hand — held it gingerly with two fingers and furiously shook it so that all of the bits and pieces of plastic attesting to Jesse's existence fell out and stared up at her obscenely from the white bedspread. Once it was empty, she pitched it away, as if it contained some inner vileness — as if it were a contaminated object that would surely destroy her if she were to hold on to it one moment longer.

The water was still running in the shower. She heard Kevin's satisfying splashing sounds. Her first impulse was to confront him with the evidence of his infidelity. She would go into the bathroom and show him the bits and pieces of Jesse that were now defiling their pure white candlewick bedspread.

But then she asked herself: What evidence do I really have? What inviolate, invincible, endurable, unassailable evidence? Without such hard evidence, Kevin would, as he had done before, offer an elaborate explanation. And it would be sound too. No gaping loopholes. She knew that unless she had a solid case against him, he would talk his way out of this situation, just as he had talked his way out of similar ones. He would then walk away feeling lightheaded, having averted by a hair's breadth another crisis in his life. Actually, with his ability to rationalize, he would think he had averted a crisis in *her* life. She would then be left with the frustration of living as she had lived throughout their marriage — in a fool's paradise, always half denying, half believing.

With one vicious swipe of her hand, Laura cleared the credit cards off the bed and watched as they skittered across the hardwood floor. She furiously brushed the bedspread, as if the spot where the stuff had lain had left an indelible dirty imprint. Her fingers still felt the imprint of the leather wallet and she was certain that all the waters of Damascus and all the waters of Israel wouldn't wash them clean. She felt like shouting, as Lady Macbeth had shouted as the blood of Macduff stained her hands, "Out, damned spot! Out, I say."

She got up and paced the floor, rapidly folding one ice cold hand into the other to quiet her agitation. She searched her mind for ways to approach Kevin, discarding first this way, then that way. And then, as if she had suddenly developed a feral cunning, she recalled what she had learned in one of her philosophy courses. She was sure it was Hume's philosophy. *When you are in a den of thieves, you must become a thief.* Then and there she decided to become a thief.

She picked up the telephone on her bedside table and placed a call to Lottie, asking her to telephone as soon as she hung up, but to ask no questions.

Lottie asked anyway. "What am I being an accomplice to now, Laura? Is it immoral, illegal or fattening?"

"None of the above," she hastily assured Lottie, trying to keep her voice airy despite her lack of time for such banter. "A domestic difference of opinion, that's all. I just want to prove a point ... You know Kevin. Unless he can place his fingers in the wound ... Just call me! Just do it!"

"Yeah! Is that right? Just call you," Lottie said, and Laura knew she would be pursing her lips to blow strands of hair from her forehead, sensing she was becoming involved in something more profound than Laura was letting on.

To forestall any further delving, Laura rushed in with a light laugh. "You know how Kevin is. He always wins because he has the facts and figures at his fingertips and I always have only a hazy recall."

Lottie hesitated for only a second or two before saying, in a playful, suspicious tone, "I don't know what you're up to, Laura, but if I go along, I hope it won't get me the electric chair."

Laura hung up and immediately readjusted the bell on the telephone upwards so that Kevin would be sure to hear it even over the running water. When Lottie called back, Laura allowed the telephone to ring several times before answering it. When she did answer, she spoke in a loud voice.

"Yes, he's home." She heard the water pipes shuddering in protest as Kevin quickly turned off the taps. "He's in the shower now." She kept her words stiff and rigid, inserting pauses at the right time. She ignored Lottie's sputtering confusion and puzzlement, and carried on her one-sided conversation.

"Yes. I see. I thought as much. Is that right? Well, it's not as much news as you think it is." She paused, as though she were absorbing what the person on the other end of the line was saying, and then she said, her mouth tight and her teeth clenched, "Don't ever call here again! Never! Never!" Then she cancelled the conversation without even saying goodbye, thinking that she would have to make up a good lie for Lottie.

Seconds later, Kevin shouted out, "In the name of God what was that all about, Laura?"

She didn't answer him. Instead, she cringed and picked the wallet up off the floor, although its very touch made her flesh burn. She stuffed the cards back into it. Then she walked into the bathroom. Kevin was fiercely towelling himself dry when she entered. "Jesse," she said in answer to his question. "That was Jesse." Her tone was noncommittal.

"Jesse?" Kevin stopped towelling immediately and modestly wrapped the towel around his loins, as though the mere mention of Jesse's name made his private parts not for her eyes. She thought of Adam and the fig leaf. She thought of guilt. And shame.

"What did he want? Why were you so nasty?"

She could hear the nervousness in his voice, although he tried to be nonchalant as he tugged at the towel to keep it in place.

She produced the open wallet with a flourish. "This," she said. "His wallet."

Kevin saw Jesse's name on the identification card. His face blanched as white as it had the day she had told him she was pregnant.

At first, he tried to bluster his way out. "We must have mixed them up in the taxi to the airport."

As was his habit, he forced anger to forestall an argument. "Don't go telling me I can't even share a taxi with the man. And I can't have him banned from going to these conferences just because you get piqued. He's entitled to go just as much as I am. And it seemed only sensible to share the cost of a taxi."

Laura held her ground. She never even flinched at the ease with which Kevin thought he could dupe her.

"That's a lie, Kevin. A bald-faced lie," she said levelly, her own lie slipping easily over her tongue. "Jesse just called. Remember? He called to say he planted the wallet hoping I'd find it. He said he was tired of pretending. He wants me to know, since you obviously don't have the guts to tell me yourself, that you've been having an affair for years now. Years and years."

She wondered whether she had overplayed her hand. Would Jesse be likely to reveal the affair? Would he say guts? Had she been correct in assuming the affair had being going on for years and years?

But as Kevin slowly lowered himself down on the edge of the tub, the most dejected human being she had ever seen, his skin turning chalky grey and his face becoming hollowed and gaunt as if it had suddenly fallen in upon itself, Laura knew she had done a masterful job. His shoulders drooped forward so that his chin almost touched his chest. He began to sob — great wracking sobs that, even in her anger and betrayal, tore at her heart. She could feel the wrench of them in her own body. It was all she could do to restrain herself from going to him and putting her arms around him and telling him — as she had that other time in his study — that everything would work out.

But this time she was sure things would not work out — at least, not in the way they had always worked out before. She felt as if her marriage — her very life — was being caught up in a swift undertow, and she was being pulled under.

Once her cunning was no longer needed to trap Kevin, there was space in her brain for other emotions. Rage and fear and sorrow and disgust all came tumbling in on her at the same time so that, even as she wanted to comfort him, she also wanted to claw at him, to call him all sorts of coarse, low-minded names: Fag! Queer! Pansy! Fruit! She even wished she had more low-minded names, but these were the extent of her alternative vocabulary for homosexual. She wanted to scream at him until her voice once again became the wail of the banshee. She felt nausea rising up in her throat. She pitched towards the toilet, holding herself upright by clutching the vanity cabinet. She jerked up the seat cover and vomited. When her stomach was emptied, she wiped her mouth and her eyes with a handful of toilet paper and staggered back to the bedroom.

Kevin followed her. As she folded into herself on the bed-spread, he mumbled over and over again, until the words were worn so smooth she couldn't hear them anymore, "I'm sorry! I'm sorry! I'm sorry!"

He sat on the bed beside her, not touching her, although she could feel that he wanted to touch her. It would help him to confess what he had to confess. "It's true," he said heavily, the weight of more than twenty years of underhandedness, artifice and deception lifting from his shoulders. "I never wanted to hurt you. Never intended to hurt you. And you must know I'd give my life rather than hurt Hannah."

For an instant, Laura wished she hadn't taken Hume's advice. She wished she had continued to allow Kevin his cover of deceit, which in turn would have allowed her the comfort of denial — or, more precisely, the comfort of *continued* denial, because to be truthful, she had learned nothing new in the past few minutes.

There had always been denial on her part, and on his part, and this abundance of denial had rotted not only their marriage, but their lives as well. It had squeezed the juice out of their very beings. It had robbed them of any lustre, any splendour.

He begged her not to leave him. For his sake. For Hannah's sake. But all she could think of was escaping from his sight. The very thought of him making love to Jesse and then coming to her bed — as he must have done on several occasions over the years — repulsed her. Her body convulsed from the thought and she staggered to the toilet once more, this time vomiting pure bile.

When she came back to the bedroom, Kevin still hadn't moved from where he sat on the edge of the bed, the towel still stretching across his middle. She went to her closet and began pulling sweaters and dresses off the hangers. She couldn't wait one more moment. She would move into the spare bedroom.

But Kevin thought she was packing to leave the house. He panicked. "You can't leave me! You can't," he wailed, grabbing her arm. "I'm in line for the Dean's job. I'll never get it if they know. Not a chance. I might even lose the Chairman's job. And, for God's sake, think about Hannah. Wait until she's through university. It'll be easier for her then."

As he rattled off the negatives, Laura realised that he must have rehearsed the horrors of discovery many times. But she didn't care. She no longer cared about saving his job or saving his pride. She flicked his arm away from her, as if her flesh burnt from his touch.

He gave her reasoned excuses, and when these didn't slow her momentum in piling clothes on the bed, he parcelled out blame. "I never wanted to get married. I tried to tell you. You wouldn't listen. You wouldn't even consider abortion. You were hell-bent on marriage.

She threw his accusation back in his face. "And you got married rather than face up to what you were — what you are. And because Father was your supervisor."

He begged for understanding, even though he knew very well she had none to give him. "Do you have any idea what it's been like for me all these years?" he implored, getting up to pace the room and, in his agitation, forgetting to clasp the towel which was slipping over his hips.

"What it's been like for you!" she parroted, her voice rising in agitation. "What do you think it's been like for me?" She never once broke stride in pulling sweaters from drawers, and hangers from closets, and furiously tossing the stuff on the bed as if she were trying to salvage her belongings from a fire. "I'm the one who had the wool pulled over her eyes. All the time thinking there must be something wrong with me. Always trying to get a corner of your affection. And here it was dear Jesse all the time. No wonder the sight of him always made me want to puke." She forced herself to add, "It has always been Jesse, hasn't it. Ever since you met him."

He stopped pacing instantly. "Yes," he admitted, his voice subdued. "But leave his name out of this. Don't put the blame on Jesse."

She pushed past him to leave the room, her arms filled with clothes, not knowing what she would do tomorrow or the next day, just moving now on instinct — the instinct that told her to be out of his sight, to be out of hearing distance of Jesse Morris' name.

"Please don't go," he pleaded, as she started for the door, the supplicating tone back in his voice. "If not for my sake, stay for Hannah's sake. For God's sake, stay long enough for ..."

Hannah's bedroom door opened and closed. Kevin broke off in mid-sentence. Laura stood riveted in the doorway. She and Kevin locked glances, each one knowing the other was hoping that Hannah hadn't heard them arguing.

Laura instantly calmed her voice and whispered that she was going to move into the spare bedroom. "I'll tell Hannah it's on account of your snoring." She stated that, as soon Hannah left for Vancouver for her summer vacation, she would move out to the cottage at Macquapit Lake. And that Kevin was not to come out there. As for what would happen in the future, she was too confused at the moment to make any permanent plans, but the fact that Hannah was intending to leave home and go to Laval

University for her second year of studies would make the separation easier for all of them.

Because living with rationed love had become almost second nature to her, the move across the hall didn't affect Laura in any emotional or sexual way. Yet she knew she couldn't continue living in such close proximity to Kevin. She would have to come up with some excuse to move out on a more permanent basis — not just to the lake in the summer. She could never again undress in Kevin's presence. She could never again take a shower while Kevin was in the house. Indeed, even the thought of her under-garments lying for all these years in bureau drawers, side by side with Kevin's shorts and pyjamas, filled her with revulsion — especially when she now knew that he had purchased these things with Jesse's pleasure in mind.

Although Laura easily convinced Hannah that she had moved into the spare bedroom because of Kevin's snoring — and although she had also been able to throw Lottie off the scent whenever her friend inquired about the need for the cloak and dagger phone call — she often wished that one of them had managed to unmask her, to uproot her lie and afterwards spread it out to dry like damp soil in the sunlight. Instead, she held it inside her, in the deep, dark places of her being, where it continued to fester — another raw wound that simply wouldn't heal.

She felt weighed down by a need to unburden herself, to tell someone her secret pain. During the day she had to force herself to laugh, to hurry her steps along the corridors, even to talk, when the talk served no obvious purpose. During the night, this need took over her dreams.

One night she dreamt she was with a group of faculty members who were on a bus going to a picnic. Through some bad guidance, they ended up in a park in downtown Boston — a park that was a hangout for unshaven men, shuffling over the ground with their overcoats, the pockets of which hid bottles of cheap liquor. And there were bag ladies, too. In their layered outfits and scraggly hair, they hovered over meagre belongings that were piled

148

in a higgledy-piggledy fashion into rusted shopping carts. And there were panhandlers who sidled up to the well-dressed faculty members and asked for handouts.

Suddenly, in her dream, all of the other faculty members disappeared and Laura was left alone. But, strangely, she wasn't afraid — actually, she was delighted. She eagerly approached each derelict, each beggar, each panhandler, and told them the story of her marriage.

"You poor woman," they all said. "What a tragic life you've led."

While this wasn't the sympathy of a nation that Mrs. LaPorte had received, it was enough to lessen the pain, and for several minutes after Laura woke up she had been able to cling to the sensation of release.

Each time she was tempted to tell Lottie how things really were, she would think about the harm the telling would do to Kevin and to Hannah — and what harm it would do to herself. And she would hold off.

Once, when she actually got as far as picking up the telephone to call Lottie to tell her everything, she stopped because she recalled an incident another teacher had related to her during a school conference they had both attended in Halifax.

Leo Buscaglia had been the keynote speaker, and Laura didn't know whether it was Buscaglia's talk on the need for love in everyone's life, or whether it was the wine that she and the other teacher, Harold, both imbibed afterwards in their hotel lounge, but the evening had become very mellow. Harold had ended up telling her about an incident from his past that had haunted him all of his life.

He had told her that he had come from well-to-do parents and, as such, had attended a very posh boys' school in Britain. As his story unfolded, she had learned that when Harold was fifteen or sixteen he had told his superiors that the custodian who was in charge of housekeeping was stealing bed linen from the stores department. His claim was checked out and found to be correct. The custodian was fired.

"And that," said Harold dejectedly, "should have been the end of the story."

However, years and years later, Harold, who by now lived in Canada, returned home to Britain and, just by happenstance, came upon the stores thief sitting on a bench in Hyde Park. The man was wearing a mission-type overcoat and had all the appearances of being down and out. Harold learned that after the man had been fired, he had never been able to get another job. Worst of all, he learned that the fellow had only taken two pillowcases and that the big-time linen thief had gotten away unscathed.

Tears had rolled down Harold's face as he related this story, and Laura finally understood why, during faculty gatherings, Harold always laughed louder and danced harder than anyone else present — and why his eyes never laughed or danced all the while he was making merry.

As she had planned, Laura moved out to Macquapit Lake the day school ended. She took with her the current literature on dyslexia, with which she wanted to become familiar. She also took a batch of addresses from universities in the southwestern United States. She intended to apply for a sabbatical and to spend it in a climate more hospitable than the one in New Brunswick, especially since the sabbatical could begin in January. In a last minute grab at the university library, and hoping that the student checking out the books wouldn't associate her name with Kevin's, she picked up several "how-to" books — how to end a marriage painlessly, how to get a divorce for mere pennies, how to start life after divorce — and a handful of other books that promised nothing more cerebral that a delightful escape from reality.

The first week at the lake went by and she didn't open even one of the books — not even one that offered escape. Nor did she apply to any universities. She walked around in a torpor. She wandered up and down the lake shore, feeling detached from, and indifferent to, everything around her. Some mornings, she took a ten-minute walk to the wild strawberry patch that adjoined her cottage lot. On each berry picking excursion she promised herself that she would convert the strawberries into a pie. However, lethargy always took over by the time she had picked a cupful. She would then walk home, sauntering across the meadow even more slowly than on the way there, eating the berries as she walked. Once home, she would sit on her front verandah and contemplate nothing more worthwhile than the anticipated idleness of the day.

By the end of her second week at the cottage, she began half-heartedly to read her self-help books. One advised that the first step in rebuilding a new life was to accept that the old one was dead. When she read this, she realized she was already one step ahead of the proposed program. Months earlier she had accepted that her marriage was dead. Indeed, years earlier she had all but fully accepted its demise. Still, she continued to read on until she learned she had no need whatsoever for the book's help. She had already arrived at the last two steps: Accept the situation and let go of the anger. She knew now that she had no desire to resurrect the marriage, even if such a possibility existed. As for her anger, whatever amount she had — and she didn't think she had an undue amount, given the circumstances — she wasn't at the moment willing to give it up, and no self-help book was going to pressure her into doing so.

One concern that dogged her was that others would blame her solely and completely for the marriage breakdown — Hannah, her parents, probably Lottie. Since she couldn't give the true reason for the separation and eventual divorce, it would seem to onlookers that she had caused the demise of the union. Another concern was that the demise of the union would cause these same people pain. Many times, she had heard her parents say that Kevin was the son they had never had. Now she was the one who was going to make him their ex-son.

Sometimes, though, in her more sardonic moments, she would tell herself that one of the more serious spin-offs from the break-up would be the severe curtailment of her mother's conversation at cocktail parties. Vera would no longer be able to say with pride, as she sipped her white wine, that her son-in-law, who was really more like a son, was now Chairman of his Department, Dean of his faculty, or President of his university, or whatever great things she had in store for Kevin. It just wouldn't carry the same clout if she had to say *ex-son-in-law*. She supposed her mother would now be forced to wait until Hannah made great strides in some profession before she had anyone else worth trotting out in drawing rooms. She couldn't imagine Vera saying — at least, not with much verve — that her daughter, her only child, was teaching long and short vowels to backward students in a junior high school.

However, what concerned Laura even more than the pain to her loved ones and the shame of being considered the one who wanted out of a perfectly good marriage, was the very real possibility that her flimsy connection with Hannah — a connection that, even in the best of times, was precariously fragile — would become totally severed. It was this possibility that filled her nights at the lake with fretful sleep and kept her days dull and heavy.

One morning in July — a Tuesday morning — when Laura had been at the lake a little over two weeks, she watched a hummingbird make delighted attacks on the fully blooming honeysuckle that straddled the lawn outside her bedroom window. The smallness of the bird, coupled with the vigour with which it attacked each bloom, made Laura think about the power of the life force that exists within each creature on the earth, no matter how small, no matter how insignificant. She took the appearance of the bird as a good omen, signifying that it was high time for her to begin to appreciate life, even if she couldn't manage to relish it. A surge of energy instantly followed.

She got out of bed, although it was a full hour earlier than her usual time to get up. She rummaged in her closet for a lightweight jogging suit and hurriedly pulled it on and then headed for the strawberry patch. This time, though, she was determined not simply to eat the berries, but to make a pie out of them. Already, she could feel the satisfying touch of the flour and shortening against the flesh of her hands. And she could feel the gratification of molding the flour and shortening and water into a pie shell.

She raced across the meadow, a plastic jug lashed by its handle to her waistband. As she came abreast of the strawberry patch, she saw that someone — a man, dressed in jeans and sweatshirt — had already beaten her to the berries. Instinctively, she slowed her pace, slightly apprehensive, trying to determine who the person was. There were only a dozen or so cottages on her side of the lake, and since most of the owners were double-income families, the occupants only came on weekends.

She cautiously moved in closer, and when she did, she saw that the berry picker was a stranger and that he had already filled a jug flush to the brim with her strawberries. The jug was overflowing and some of the berries had spilled over, and these he was arranging on a cloth that he had spread on the ground.

Hesitant, but too curious to head back without finding out what was going on, Laura moved in still closer.

The stranger looked up and saw her.

"Oops!" he said, jumping to his feet from his stooping position. "I hope you're not the strawberry patch police."

She noticed that his English was heavily accented with French, and because she was somewhat vexed that he was encroaching on her property, she replied crisply, "Not exactly. But I am the strawberry patch owner. And who are you?"

He exaggeratedly wiped his brow, as if he had just escaped a chain gang round-up. "Whew!" he said, a smile in his voice. "Is that better or worse than being the police ... I mean you being the owner?" He added quickly, pointing to the picked strawberries, "You can have these back. I just wanted to paint them." For confirmation, he looked towards his easel. "I like to capture ..."

Then, as if he realized he had gone on too long with his explanation and still hadn't identified himself, he stopped short and said, "I'm Claude Frenette. I just moved into my Aunt Muriel's cottage — Muriel Frenette." He gestured to his right. "That cottage over there." He extended his hand to Laura.

Laura instantly relaxed and moved towards him. She should have guessed who he was the instant she had seen him. She had been told he was coming. She smiled widely and extended her own hand, saying mischievously, "Then you must be 'My young nephew — the artist from Montreal — who is going to be living in our cottage next summer because we're off to visit Henri's brother in Calgary.'"

Claude clasped her hand and laughed. "You've sure got Aunt Muriel down pat." He added, still with a hint of laughter in his voice, "And that must make you 'The nice people in the cottage two doors up.'"

Laura gave a light, easy laugh. "Well, I'm one of the nice people, anyway. I'm Laura. The rest of the nice people have other things to do this summer. My husband has too much work to take off the time. And my daughter has gone to Vancouver to visit her grandparents."

"Sure glad you came, Laura," Claude said, indicating with his hand the wide expanse of meadows and lake. "I like peace and quiet, but this is almost too much. I thought I was going to have to invent a man Friday."

Laura noticed that his French pronunciation of her name — *Laure* — instantly removed its severity. She had always felt it was better suited to a woman of the Quaker persuasion than to a person of her make-up.

She noticed, too, the permanent laugh lines around Claude's eyes, the sprinkling of grey in his hair. She said, without thinking, "I guess I don't have your aunt down as pat as you think I do. I got the impression you were young."

Realizing she was saying he was old, she hastily amended, "I mean, seventeen or eighteen. That kind of young. When we were boarding up our places last fall, Muriel said her young nephew was coming this summer and I instantly imagined an eighteen-year-old, and hearty partying going on all summer long. My ears being blasted with rap music and that sort of thing."

Again she blustered, "I didn't mean to ... She just kept saying my young nephew ... I just assumed ..."

Claude laughed away her embarrassment. "I s'pose when you're seventy, forty-one probably seems young enough to be called 'my young nephew.'"

"That's true," she agreed easily, and began to relax. "My daughter — she's eighteen — she thinks forty is being on the verge of needing the pine box."

Claude, remembering that he had practically picked her strawberry patch clean, pointed to the overflowing jug. "About the berries. I could drop them in to you on my way back. That's if you can spare them for a couple of hours?"

Laura's eyes followed Claude's to the jug, and then, surprising herself with her brashness, she struck a bargain with him. "If you'll agree to immortalize these berries on canvas I'll promise to make a memorable pie out of them. And I'll give you half. To welcome you to the neighbourhood."

She pointed to her cottage. "I guess you know my cottage — it's that green place with the white shutters. And the brown Toyota in the driveway."

On the way back to the cottage, she walked much faster than she ordinarily would have done. And, as she walked, she kept hearing the soft way Claude had pronounced her name. And she kept seeing his eyes. They were the deep blue colour of the lake. She had noticed, too, that when he laughed, his eyes laughed. She liked that about a man — about anyone. She had always hoped that Hannah's eyes would be like that. But Hannah's were more like Kevin's — sober, scholarly eyes, too serious for nonsensical laughter. She felt certain that if Mary/Joseph had lived, his eyes would have flashed and danced with every smile.

She regretted that she had only a couple of hours to get ready for Claud's visit — two hours to shower, wash her hair, tidy up her kitchen and make two pie crusts. And she regretted that she hadn't taken better care of herself over the past several weeks. She surveyed her baggy jogging suit and ran her hands over her tangled mess of hair. As she hurried along, her mind searched her clothes closet for her coral cotton blouse and matching striped shorts. She hoped she had brought that outfit along because coral enhanced her tan and brought out the sun streaks in her brown hair. She liked her hair in summer, mostly because her father had always liked it then. He used to say that after the sun got at her hair it reminded him of the iced tea her mother brewed on hot days. He would say this very same thing every summer, just as soon as her mother had placed the glass jar of tea on the verandah to steep. Because he was a man to whom compliments didn't come easily, she had always treasured this one and took very good care of her hair so as not to make a liar of him when the iced tea was put out on the verandah.

Claude arrived with the berries in an earthenware jug that she recognized as the one his aunt Muriel had used to hold wildflowers. By the time he came, she had everything in readiness except the pastry. As she held the screen door wide so that it wouldn't brush against the jug of berries, he confessed that the jug wasn't as full as when she had last seen it because he had snitched a few as he walked across the meadow.

Laughing, she owned up that she always did the same thing, arriving home with only half as many berries as she had started out with. She invited him in for coffee and then admitted that the pie crust hadn't materialized.

"I'll have it to you by supper time. I promise." She indicated the cleared-off counters and the fresh cloth on the table. "I had to dig this place out," she confessed. "Living alone, you let things pile up."

Laura learned that morning that Claude was married and that his wife, Leah, had muscular dystrophy. Sometimes, he said, she was confined to a wheelchair. He got away most summers for a couple of months because either Leah's mother or his came in to look after Leah. He said that both mothers, as well as Leah, insisted that for the sake of his art he needed to have some unencumbered time to himself.

In turn, Claude learned that Laura was coming to grips with a foundering marriage, although the details of the foundering were left undiscussed.

"Children?" Laura asked, as she passed Claude a plate of store-bought cookies. He shook his head, a little sadly she thought. "Afraid not. We didn't want to put stress on Leah's health." He looked at her over the steaming coffee. "And you? Children? I mean other than your daughter."

"No. Like I said — a daughter, Hannah. She started university here last year, but now she wants to transfer to Laval. Don't exactly know why. Except to improve her French. And probably to get away from home. Although she was never one to strain at

156

the leash. Right now she's out in Vancouver visiting her grandparents — that's my parents. They retired out there."

That evening, when Laura took the freshly baked pie to Claude's cottage, he was just leaving to walk the lake shore. He came to the door wearing jeans, windbreaker and running shoes.

"So it's pay-up time," he joked, stepping aside and motioning her to come in. "I'll make you a cup of coffee to go with this." He then noticed that she, too, was dressed in jeans, windbreaker and running shoes. He pointed to his feet. "I'm ready to walk the shore. Why don't you join me?" He nodded towards the pie that she was still holding. "That'll keep."

They walked along the shore, just inches from the water, and she told him that her favourite time of day at the cottage was dusk. "I love those minutes just before night takes over," she said, waving her hand to indicate the shoreline with its jagged rocks jutting out here and there and the half-dead trees leaning out over the water. "I love the way the rough edges of the shoreline become blurred and everything appears soft and formless." She pointed to some trees that had been gnawed bare by the spruce budworm. "Even those appear velvety. You can't really tell that most of the needles are gone. And there's a gentleness about. The wind usually dies down. And the water becomes calm. It's like an Impressionist painting."

He said he liked the evenings best, too. Evenings were good for dreaming, but mornings were best for his art.

He talked to her about his work, about how he liked capturing objects in light and shadow and how he tried to always keep a balance between reality and illusion. She didn't comprehend everything he was saying, never having painted, but she liked the fact that he talked to her as if she did comprehend everything.

That first evening's walk set in motion a pattern of evening walks that was to last for the next month and a half. It was well over two weeks later that she told him the truth about the break-up of her marriage. She told him about it as they picked their way over the rocky shore.

"When I found out that Kevin was a homosexual, I almost wished him dead," she said, surprising herself by saying the word so effortlessly now, when it had seemed so foreign and outlandish to her just a few weeks ago. In fact, she could say it almost matter-of-factly now, as if she were saying, "When I found out that Kevin was a diabetic." She admitted her desire for Kevin's death shamefacedly. "I saw it as the only way out. No disgrace for anyone. Not for him. Not for Hannah. Not for me."

She shrugged. "Of course, I'm coming to grips with the situation now. Except for Hannah's part in it. She still doesn't know. And I worry about that. She adores her father. I wouldn't want it to change things for her."

Claude didn't seemed shocked at her admission that she had wished Kevin dead, and when she told him how guilty she felt over wishing this, he reminded her that she had only *almost* wished him dead — not actually wished him dead. He told her it was natural that she would have felt as she did. "You felt trapped in Kevin's problem, so that it became your problem. And there's nothing more frustrating than being a helpless bystander, an onlooker to someone else's problems."

She had wondered then whether he was talking about his own marriage, especially when he added, "You want to fix things. To make things as they were. Or, at least, the way you wish they had been. But the person you want to fix has either accepted that things can't be fixed, or doesn't see anything needing to be fixed. So you just stand there frustrated and helpless."

Several days later, when he asked her if she had had any inkling about Kevin's homosexuality — if there had been any signs that she could only now recognize — she admitted there were lots and quoted from her Sunday school teachings to show that she simply hadn't been willing to see them. "You know how it goes, 'There's none so blind as those who will not see.'" She admitted that only lately had she come to realize that she had not wanted to see the signs.

She described one action of Kevin's that had always perplexed her, but which now, in hindsight, made sense. Whenever

Kevin would leave for work, she would watch him unnoticed from the front room window. He had always done the same thing as soon as he settled himself behind the wheel of the car. He would reach up and twist the rearview mirror so that he had a good view of himself. He would then rearrange his cowlick of hair so that it fell over his forehead in what she felt was a sexy tousled sort of way — the way it fell naturally when he was fixing the stopped-up sink or correcting papers. Since he obviously hadn't been doing this to captivate her, she now believed he had been preening himself in preparation for seeing his lover.

On another evening, around dusk, Laura and Claude walked further than usual — long enough to allow the wind to die down and to make talking easier — and she told him about Mary/Joseph.

"I told you I only have one child. But I had two. And sometimes I still think I have two. He's still that much with me."

She told Claude how this child had come to be called Mary/Joseph, and how she had always believed that she would have felt less lonely had he lived.

"Perhaps I've only been deluding myself," she admitted, not wanting Claude to confirm whether she had or hadn't been deluding herself, "but I always felt that if Mary/Joseph had lived he would have changed the dynamics of our family so that I wouldn't always have thought of myself as clinging to its edges. He would have been there for me when Hannah and Kevin shut me out, or when I perceived that they had shut me out." She stooped down then, picked up a flat stone and skipped it across the lake. When she heard the last skip on the water, she finished her musings. "And it would have been better for Hannah, too. She would have had to share Kevin and maybe she wouldn't have been so possessive of him." She then shrugged and became relentlessly honest. "Or maybe I wouldn't have created an environment where she felt she had to be possessive."

They had been walking side by side, but still separately. Now, Claude encircled her with his arm and pulled her close, giving her a gentle, warm hug. "For all sad words of tongue and pen," he said softly, quoting from Whittier, "the saddest are these, 'It might have been!'"

Then, quickly, in case she thought he was censuring her for dreaming dreams, he confessed that he, too, had often indulged in might-have-beens and what-ifs. He said that he sometimes wondered if his marriage stayed intact because of Leah's sickness, rather than in spite of it. He told her that Leah had been studying to be a lawyer before she became sick and he often wondered whether, if she had gone on and become a successful professional, she would have remained content with a struggling artist. And he also wondered whether, if they had had children, the dynamics of the marriage would be different from what they now were.

That same evening, Laura told Claude that she had become a teacher by default. She described the circumstances that had culminated in her teaching in a junior high school.

"For all that, though," she said quickly, in her own defense, "I'm a good teacher. I not only know it in my bones, but from what the students say." She laughed a small, wry laugh. "I think I empathize with them and they sense it. I know they'd prefer doing something else — almost anything else — rather than being in that classroom. And so would I. So I try to make the day as profitable and as pleasant as possible for all of us."

She confessed, laughing, that there were some days when she shouldn't be allowed near a classroom. And she admitted that often she got so frustrated, she had difficulty being patient. "I teach students who have reading difficulties," she explained. "So I have to be so careful with them. So patient. Their egos are already bruised enough without my adding more black and blue marks." She sighed, hating to admit that there were many times when she wasn't as patient as she ought to be. "There are times," she said, "times when I get so frustrated ... Like one day just before school ended, I was writing a homework assignment on the board for the grade seven class, and they kept asking me if it would be all right if they copied the assignment in ballpoint pen, or in pencil, and if it was all right to write it on borrowed paper if they had forgotten their notebooks. And if they could print if they couldn't write. They sort of panic when they have to do anything that deals with words," she explained, "so they stall for time. So this day I kept saying, yes, it's fine to write it with pencil or pen, or in their notebooks or, if they didn't have their notebooks, to borrow some paper. Or print the letters, if that's what they wanted. By that time, I had said 'yes, that would be fine,' so many times I thought that the next time someone asked me if it would be all right to use pencil instead of ballpoint, I was going to scream, 'Write it in blood, for all I care. Stencil it with your toenails.' Afterwards, I thought, 'Girl, you're losing it. Next thing you'll be rushing around the classroom ripping up paper, and throwing things helter-skelter like a mad scientist.'

Claude stopped walking and laughed, a hearty bent-over type of laugh, making her shortcomings as a teacher seem not so terrible.

A few minutes later, when he was helping Laura climb over some slippery rocks that blocked the shoreline, he asked, "And what would you have preferred doing rather than teaching?" He asked this in a way that allowed her to acknowledge to herself what she had always wanted for her life.

"Journalism. I always wanted to be a writer of some sort — mostly a journalist. Just like you always wanted to paint. I guess that's why I admire you so much for carrying through with it. I let other things get in the way. So I still feel a twinge of envy when I see someone — especially a woman — on the television, reporting from Beirut or Moldavia or wherever. I think, that could have been me. I picture myself with sun-baked dust on my face, my hair blowing this way and that way and the tail of my shirt half-in and half-out over my jeans, because what I'm saying is more important than how I look."

By this time, the sun had dipped into the horizon, leaving behind ribbons of pinks and mauves and reds. Because she didn't want Claude to think she was wallowing in self-pity, she cut short her talking and pointed to the sky. "Look over there. At the sky across the lake. It looks like you just cleaned your brushes on its surface."

They kept on walking, and soon a bright, fully rounded moon appeared, and the water became so still she could barely hear it lapping against the shore. They reached for each others' hands.

She was not certain who reached first, or whether it just resulted from an accidental brushing up against each other. The touching was shy and hesitant at first, then more sure. When she asked him how he coped with his wife's illness, he gently hilled and daled the air with his free hand, like an airplane dipping its wings. "Some days are stones." He had added, "A lot of days are stones."

He was quiet for a long time after that, as if he were tallying up the days that were diamonds and the ones that were stones and then placing them into separate columns. When he spoke, his voice was compassionate. "It's hard for me, but it's a lot worse for Leah. Sometimes she has remissions, although these are getting more and more scarce. But each time she has one, I foolishly keep thinking that this one will last." He sighed heavily, "But it never does."

She learned during that walk that Claude's marriage was now filled with duty and care — that, long ago, the passion had been lost in medicines and despair; that his wife still loved him enough to try and convince him to divorce her; and that he still loved her enough to stand by her, no matter how rough the going got. He said it was unfortunate that the sickness had begun shortly after the honeymoon so that during the hard times neither of them had memories of a normal marriage to fall back upon.

A sudden wind came up and Laura hunched her shoulders to keep out the chill. When she gave a slight shiver, he encircled her waist and pulled her close to him, anchoring her hand in his. His thigh brushed hers, jeans against jeans, and she could feel the heat from that contact point warming her whole body. She felt as if she had been pulled into a safe, snug harbour — a place where she would never again feel lonely. She felt fragile and protected — and seductively female. She scandalized herself by being delighted because underneath her jeans and sweater and red anorack she was wearing her new ivory-coloured, satin underwear. And she was glad her hair was freshly washed and that she had buffed and polished her fingernails.

When they reached her cottage, he kissed her. He gently brushed her hair back from her face and kissed her forehead. It was just a brush of his lips, but when she didn't pull away, he moved down her face and placed a warm, full kiss on her mouth.

"I've been wanting to do that ever since I saw you looking at me across the patch of strawberries," he told her moments later. "You looked so tentative and unsure, like a timid but inquisitive little animal who wanted to come closer, but was already thinking it was folly to have come as close as it had."

Later that night, long after Claude had gone home, as Laura was getting ready for bed, she was very careful about washing her teeth, not wanting to get water on her lips in case she wiped the kiss away. And she was sure that she would never get to sleep because the places on her flesh where he had touched her — her arms and face and hair — were so alive that they demanded her wide awake attention. It was then that she finally understood why her mother hadn't washed her hand after accidently brushing it against her Donald MacPhail's fingers.

Claude had said that he would call for her the following evening, and she lay awake wishing she could make time gallop through the next twenty-four hours.

Towards the end of August, on an afternoon so hot and sultry that she couldn't concentrate on any of the chores she had placed on her list that day, Laura took a blanket and spread it on the grass in the backyard, behind a bank of pink and purple lupins. She then stretched out full-length on the blanket, so that her bare legs could soak up the sun. She closed her eyes and began daydreaming that Claude was beside her. She imagined curling into him and sliding her hands under his paint-stained tee-shirt. She imagined snaring her fingers in his hair, feeling the silkiness of it as it slid over her flesh. And she imagined Claude making love to her. She allowed her mind to linger on this last thought, encouraging it to tarry while she wondered what it would be like, just once in her life, to have her fill of love and to never again have it rationed out because the best and the most had to be kept for someone else.

As she was deep into these thoughts, a shadow fell over her closed eyelids. She heard a dull clicking sound. Startled, she sat upright and found Claude crouched beside her, holding his camera.

"I'm sorry," he said very quickly as she looked at him, confusion registering in her eyes. "I didn't mean to disturb you." He gestured with the camera. "I needed a picture. For a painting. I was afraid if I didn't get one now you might go into town and I'd never get one."

Although he spoke lightly, Laura heard something grave in his voice, as if the picture was only an excuse for whatever news he had to tell her.

Her body, sensing alarm, stiffened. "What's wrong?" She pointed at the camera, every nerve in her body suddenly on edge. She knew he only took photographs when the subject was fleeting and changing and he wanted to capture the moment to paint later — like sunrises and sunsets. And rainbows. "Why do you need a picture right away?" she asked, wishing he would laugh at her agitation. "Besides, you said I would sit for you for a painting."

He began fidgeting with the camera in the hope it would allow him to dodge an answer.

She persisted, "Something is wrong!" By now her voice was so filled with dread it came out sounding high and shrill. "I know there is. I can feel it. Tell me what it is."

He laid the camera down and took both of her hands in his. "Mother's had a bit of an attack." He hurried to reassure her. "Nothing serious. But she's in the hospital. Leah's mother is out of town. So there's no one to look after Leah. I have to go back."

"When?" She could barely say the word, but she had to know.

"In a couple of hours. I'll drive all night."

He saw the stricken look on her face and he pulled her to him. He skimmed his fingers down her cheek, along her neck and throat. He touched her as if she were a precious, fragile creature. She felt her flesh burn, hotter than the sun.

"I love you, Laura," he suddenly whispered, as if he had been hoarding the word for a long time. He touched her hair with his lips. "So wholeheartedly. So totally. More than I ever knew it was possible to love."

He tenderly smoothed her hair back from her forehead, while he continued to cradle her in his arms. "I was watching you lying there," he said. "You looked so peaceful, I wasn't sure I had the heart to tell you I had to leave. Or even if I have the strength to leave."

She clung desperately to him, sure that if she were to let go he would leave her and she would never see him again. The years of emotional impoverishment, the years that had been so arid and parched and wind whipped, flashed into her mind. "You can't leave!" she said, fiercely clutching the back of his shirt. "I won't let you. I won't." She began to sob.

He rocked her back and forth in his arms, voicing soothing words until the sobbing stopped. Then, as if all along this had been part of their plan, he very gently picked her up and carried her into the cottage and laid her on her bed. All the while he undressed her, she never said a word, just mutely watched him as he removed first her tee-shirt and then her shorts, and finally her panties and bra.

She lay naked and quiet on the bed and her eyes roved over his body as he took off his own clothes — the brown sandals that she joked made him look spiritual, the paint-spattered tee-shirt she loved because it was so uniquely him, and the jeans that seemed molded to his body. She watched as he moved towards her and then she closed her eyes and waited for his beautiful tanned body to connect with hers. Her whole being rippled with anticipation, and when she felt his flesh on her flesh it was as though their bodies had merged into one — the singer and the song, the dancer and the dance, the lover and the love.

No longer was she a lonely stranger walking the edges of other people's lives.

When Claude went back to his cottage to finish packing, Laura hurriedly showered and got dressed into her "walking the shore" clothes. She didn't want to be around to see him leave. She had to pass his cottage on the way and she tucked a note in his door so he would be sure to see it when he left. It read:

My Darling,
In the soft moments of each day, when the wind is quiet and
the sun is gentle, I'll think of you and wish you well.

Laura.

Although she walked the shore to forget that he was leaving, she couldn't manage to forget for a single second. And, as she walked, picking her way over the rocky shore, she held tight to the feel of him, the smell of him, the look of him. She felt a spiritual fullness she had never known before. It was as if his love had annointed her. She was able to forgive her father and mother for loving each other so much that she wasn't needed in their lives. She was able to forgive Hannah for preferring Kevin over her. She was able to forgive Kevin his many ruses in order to meet with Jesse. She was even able to forgive herself for pretending not to have known they were ruses.

As she walked along, she recalled Claude's love-filled voice telling her, as they had lain naked in each others arms, that as much as he loved her, he could never leave Leah to be with her.

"That's why," he had said, anguish in every word, "it's probably for the best that I have to go home. I can't grasp happiness at the expense of someone else. And you can't either. We're just not careless people."

"Like Tom and Daisy," she had said, reminding him of a conversation they had had one evening about The Great Gatsby.

"Like Tom and Daisy," he had echoed. "Careless with other people's love. You and I, we're doomed to be the Nick's and Jay's of this world."

Claude's letter was waiting for her when she returned. Like her note, it had been stuck in the edge of her screen door.

My Precious Laura,
I leave, but my heart and soul remain. You know how to
contact me through the art gallery on St. Catherine's Street
if you ever get to Montreal. I would dearly love to see you.
Be that journalist you've always wanted to be. One day I

166

will turn on the television and there you will be, in your red anorack, dust from sun-baked roads covering your face, and your hair unkempt because the tragedy that is unfolding around you is all that is important to you. When that day arrives, I will know you were real and that this summer was not a dream. I intend to paint the picture of you amongst the lupins. I might even title it, "Laura in Love." I will exhibit it, but I will never sell it. I'm convinced, Dear Laura, we were born for the summer of '91. We were born for each other.

Forever,
Claude.

T e n

The highway construction that Hannah had run into several miles back has continued on without a break. Indeed, it now has become so congested that she is forced to funnel the car into a narrow, one-way lane that is marked with sand barrels painted in highway orange.

Because the air is filled with dust from the heavy machinery, Hannah rolls up her window. But no sooner is it rolled up than the heat in the car becomes so stifling that she takes one hand from the wheel and grabs a handful of her hair and uses it to fan her neck.

"Why haven't you got air conditioning in this thing?" she demands, casting a disgruntled look at the bottom of the dashboard, where an air conditioner would ordinarily be. "Dad has an air conditioner in his car." Her voice holds blame, as if Laura, with her mind focussed on less important things, neglected to have the car properly equipped.

Laura is tempted to snap that, if Hannah feels that way, she should have asked her father to drive her. Instead, she explains, "I only drive to and from school in this thing. It would have been a big expense for nothing."

The passing mention of her father makes Hannah forget for the moment about the heat. She asks, as though the question has been on her mind since she was told of the divorce, "What's going to happen to him? Will he be okay?"

"Of course he will," Laura returns, her tone short. "How come you never ask whether I'll be okay?"

Hannah shrugs her shoulders indifferently. "I s'pose it's because you'll have your artist to look after you."

"I certainly won't," Laura says defensively. "I'll be on my own."

Hannah doesn't believe her. "Why won't he be with you? From the tone of that letter I'd say he was going to be ..."

"He's married," Laura cuts in, deciding she is sick and tired of always dealing in half-truth. "His wife is an invalid. Has been for years and years. He told me ..."

Hannah claps her hand to her ear to shut out further details of Claude's life. "I don't want to hear that stuff, Mother. Just keep it to yourself."

"Okay. If that's what you want. I thought you wanted to know."

"Not likely. Not in this lifetime," Hannah retorts and then jolts Laura by saying quickly, "But there is something I do want to know." She pauses, as if considering whether she really does want to know. She stammers, "I mean ... If I asked you something ... If it was about Dad, would you give me the truth. Not just lies masked in truth. The real truth. Not just shit like I usually get."

If Hannah expects to be reprimanded for her vulgarity, Laura disappoints her. "I won't give you shit," she says honestly. "But I won't give you anything else either. You know my motto: 'Render unto Caesar the things that are Caesar's.' So, go ask your father whatever it is you want to know about him. Ask me whatever it is you want to know about me."

"Does your motto apply to Jesse Morris, too?"

"In spades!"

Hannah hunches and unhunches her shoulders, as if she is saying more than she had ever planned to say. She confesses, "I always disliked him — Jesse Morris." She takes her hand from the wheel and rubs the back of her neck.

"I always had this creepy feeling in the back of my neck whenever his name was mentioned. Whenever Dad brought his name up, or whenever he called, I'd feel this prickle in my spine. And sometimes, when Dad would be driving me somewhere, I'd get the feeling that Jesse had been in the car only minutes before. Even though I wouldn't even know he was in the city. Sometimes I'd even say to Dad, just casual like, 'Was Jesse Morris in Fredericton today?' And he'd say, just as casual, 'Yes, he had some work at the university.' And then he'd ask, 'Did you see him someplace?' And I'd say that, no, I was just asking. And we'd let it go at that."

Hannah heaves a heavy sigh, clutches the steering wheel with both hands and settles into the seat, as if she has come home after a long journey. "I want you to know this. I was glad that you were jealous of Jesse Morris. Because I was, too. But I was always so eager to please Dad I just pretended to myself I wasn't jealous of Jesse, because he was Dad's friend. And I pretended to myself that the problem was with you, not with Jesse. That way, it made things easier for me." She finishes lamely, "I don't know if what I'm saying makes any sense or not, but it's the truth."

Laura reaches over and touches Hannah's arm, this time not expecting to be rebuffed. "It makes perfect sense to me." What she says next has nothing to do with either Kevin or Jesse Morris. It just seems the right time to say it. "It's not easy being an only child, Hannah. It's an awful burden for one pair of shoulders. Ask me, I know."

Hannah's lip trembles. "I used to long for an older brother. I really wish that Mary/Joseph had lived." She gives a wry grin. "But not with that name. Better for him to be called Sue."

Laura smiles a small smile, but makes no comment.

Hesitantly, Hannah asks her last question, "Do you hate Dad? For ..." She searches for the right word and, not finding it, says, "For everything?"

Laura shakes her head. "Not now. Not anymore."

"Because of that artist, you don't?"

Laura shakes her head again. "I don't think so. He helped. I'm certain of that. But I pressured your father into marrying me. And that was wrong. I have to face up to my own wrongs."

She quickly reaches out and presses Hannah's arm again. "But one good thing came of the marriage. Without it, there wouldn't have been you." She then says, as if the thought suddenly

170

popped into her mind, "And if I were you, I'd write a long letter to your father. Ask him whatever you want to ask him. Get at the truth. You both deserve that."

Hannah nods, as if she is confirming to herself the merit of what Laura has said. She then asks quickly, without looking at her mother, almost as if she is embarrassed by the asking, "Why don't you stay with me tonight instead of at the hotel. My roomie won't be back until tomorrow. You could have my bed. I'd take hers. She wouldn't mind."

Laura's eyes again fill with tears. This time, though, she savours them. For a moment she is tempted to take Hannah up on her offer, but then she remembers how it was when she was a freshman, how much there had been to talk about after a weekend's absence, and how little she would have wanted her mother around.

"That's really very generous of you, dear," she says, her voice warm. "Especially since I know how much you like having the room to yourself." She then gives other reasons why it would be best if she stayed in the motel. "Unfortunately, the motel's already paid for. I did it through the Fredericton motel — with Visa, so they'd be sure to hold it for me. And, besides, I intend to get a headstart in the morning. I'll want to be on the road by seven. No point in disturbing you at that hour. Especially since you don't have a class until eleven."

When Hannah looks disappointed, Laura says brightly, "I hope you realize I'm expecting a visit from you down South at March break. Wherever I decide to go. You'll be going back home in the summer, so I'd like to have you all to myself for a few days." She looks behind her at the boxes and suitcases stuffed into every inch of space. "And as soon as we get you unpacked we can have supper together. I might even take you up on the offer of dormitory food."

As soon as they arrive at Hannah's dormitory, they begin unpacking the boxes and suitcases from the back seat and then lugging the stuff up to her room. When this chore is finished, they go to supper at the residence dining hall. After a last round of goodbyes, Laura heads to her motel room. Because she intends to get a head start on the traffic in the morning, as soon as she gets to the motel she opens up her overnight bag and takes out the clothes she intends to wear the next day — underwear, jeans instead of shorts because the forecast says the temperature is going to drop, a loose sweater because she hates driving with tight sleeves, and her red anorack in case it gets colder than the forecast says it will. She lays these out on the adjoining bed.

After she closes the suitcase, the thought crosses her mind that the clothes she intends to wear in the morning are the same ones she had worn on the evening when Claude first kissed her. Immediately on the heels of this thought there is another one — she is less than a four-hour drive from Montreal. Indeed, the swiftness with which this thought enters her mind makes her wonder whether all along she has harboured the notion of continuing on to Montreal from Quebec City, and whether this is the real reason she refused Hannah's offer of shared lodgings. If she were going to Montreal, she would want to leave much earlier than if she were going back home. She would want to leave early enough so as to be in Montreal before the traffic became too heavy — early enough for Hannah to become suspicious that she wasn't driving back to Fredericton.

That she has already worked out the logistics involved in this change of plans confirms for her that going on to Montreal has been in the back of her mind all along. She even has it all thought out — how she is going to tell the school that she won't be in for the rest of the week: As soon as she arrives in Montreal and lines up a hotel room, she will call Mr. Stangroom. She will not lie in detail because she always trips herself up when she attempts to do this. Besides, she has sworn off lies. She will simply say that something unexpected has come up and she needs the extra days. She knows it really won't matter what excuse she offers him, he won't believe her anyway. Even if she were in hospital, screened off to die, even if he could hear her death rattle, he still wouldn't believe her. Monday or Friday absences always make him suspicious. She

172

recklessly tells herself that since she has already sinned by being absent on one end of the week, she might as well sin by being absent on the other.

She goes to bed hoping to get a good night's sleep. But she only sleeps in fits and start. She vacillates between driving to Montreal and going back to Fredericton. Every time she shuts her own eyes, she sees Leah's eyes — the eyes she had seen in a photograph in Claude's wallet, trusting eyes that had looked out at her from a wheelchair. When this happens, she decides to forget about Montreal and go back to Fredericton. But then, superimposed over Leah's eyes, she sees Claude's eyes — gentle eyes that had looked down into hers with love and passion and delight. She then tells herself that she cannot allow the summer of '91 to end as it did. In light and illusion. In tears. In resignation. In wistfullness. She tells herself she cannot allow it to end at all. She decides to go to Montreal.

When day breaks, she gets up, showers, dresses and, without bothering with breakfast, heads for Montreal. She drives for almost an hour, and with each minute and each mile she assures herself that she has made the right choice. She asks herself plaintively, whenever doubt starts to creep in, "When again will the passions of a man fit so rapturously with the passions of a woman?"

Just as she is beginning to be comfortable with her decision, she remembers what Claude had said to her about careless people. It's as if his voice is close to her ear. "We're not careless people, you and I. We're the Nick's and Jay's of this world."

She sees an exit sign that will take her back onto the highway to Fredericton. Almost before she realizes what she is doing, she moves into the off ramp and heads back north.

On the drive back home she tells herself she will grab hold of the remainder of her life and shape it as she has always wanted to. She will give up her sabbatical leave and her study grant. And she will give up teaching long vowels and short vowels. She will become the journalist she has always wanted to be. She can almost smell the dusty, baked smell of unpaved roads. She can almost hear Pamela Wallin saying, "Now reporting to us live from the war-ravaged countryside of ..."

But, first, she will etch the past summer on paper, just as Claude had etched it on canvas. She will make the pages talk and laugh and cry. She will preserve those evenings when they walked the rocky shore of Macquapit Lake — in words, in phrases, in sentences simple and compound. She will immortalize them in long and short paragraphs, in long and short vowels.

With her future settled, Laura reaches down to switch on the radio and notices that Hannah has forgotten her tapes. She picks one up at random and pushes it into the tape deck. Music from *Cats* once more fills the car, picking up where it had left off when Hannah had become bored with the melody and changed tapes.

She rolls down the window and lets the wind blow through her hair. She begins to sing along with the music: *"Daylight, I must wait for the sunrise, I must think of a new life. And I mustn't give in."*